YAM

BITE-SIZE CHUNKS

COREY BARBA

YAM: BITE-SIZE CHUNKS ©2008 COREY BARBA.
EDITED BY CHRIS STAROS
PUBLISHED BY TOP SHELF PRODUCTIONS, PO BOX 1282,
MARIETTA, GA 30061-1282, USA. PUBLISHERS: BRETT WARNOCK
AND CHRIS STAROS. TOP SHELF PRODUCTIONS® AND THE TOP SHELF
LOGO ARE REGISTERED TRADEMARKS OF TOPSHELF PRODUCTIONS, INC.
ALL RIGHTS RESERVED. NO PART OF THIS PUBLICATION MAY BE
REPRODUCED WITHOUT PERMISSION, EXCEPT FOR SMALL EXCERPTS
FOR PURPOSES OF REVIEW. VISIT OUR ONLINE CATALOG AT
WWW.TOPSHELFCOMIX.COM. FIRST PRINTING, JULY 2008.
PRINTED IN CANADA AT LEBONFON.

ISBN 978-1-60309-014-8
1. CHILDREN'S BOOKS
2. NICKELODEON MAGAZINE
3. GRAPHIC NOVELS

THE FOLLOWING YAM COMICS
PREVIOUSLY APPEARED IN
NICKELODEON MAGAZINE:

• "I HAIR FLOWERS": SEPTEMBER 2003
• "FLOWER POWER": (IN A TINY MARGINAL
  STRIP VERSION): MAY 2005
• "A YAM & GATO YARN": NOVEMBER 2005
• "TV DREAMS": MARCH 2007

BE SURE TO CHECK OUT:
NICKMAG.COM/COMICS

FOR: JOY, HOPE AND RAIN.

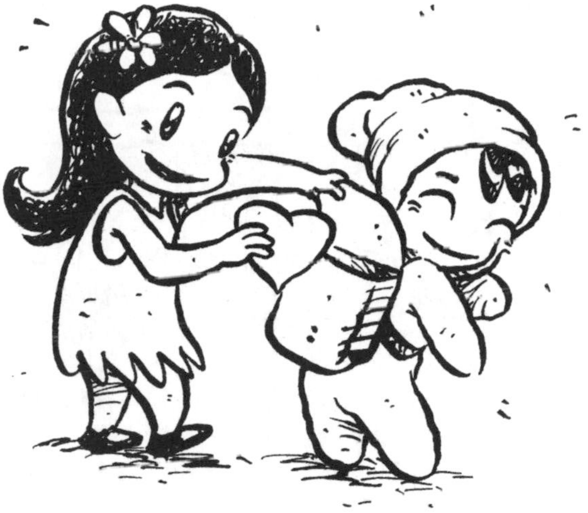

BIG CHUNKY THANKS TO:

BRETT WARNOCK AND CHRIS STAROS AT TOPSHELF, CHRIS DUFFY AND DAVE ROMAN AT NICK MAG, JOSE GARIBALDI, 3 MEN & A PEN, AND LAST BUT NOT LEAST... MOM, JENNY AND UNCLE JIM. OH, WAIT... AND THIS GUY

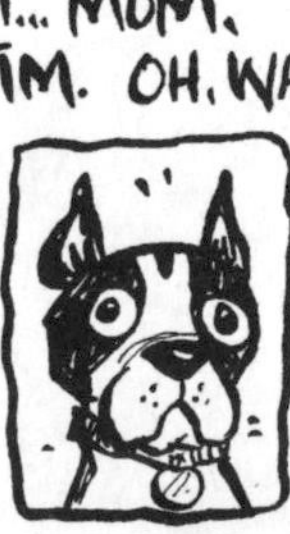

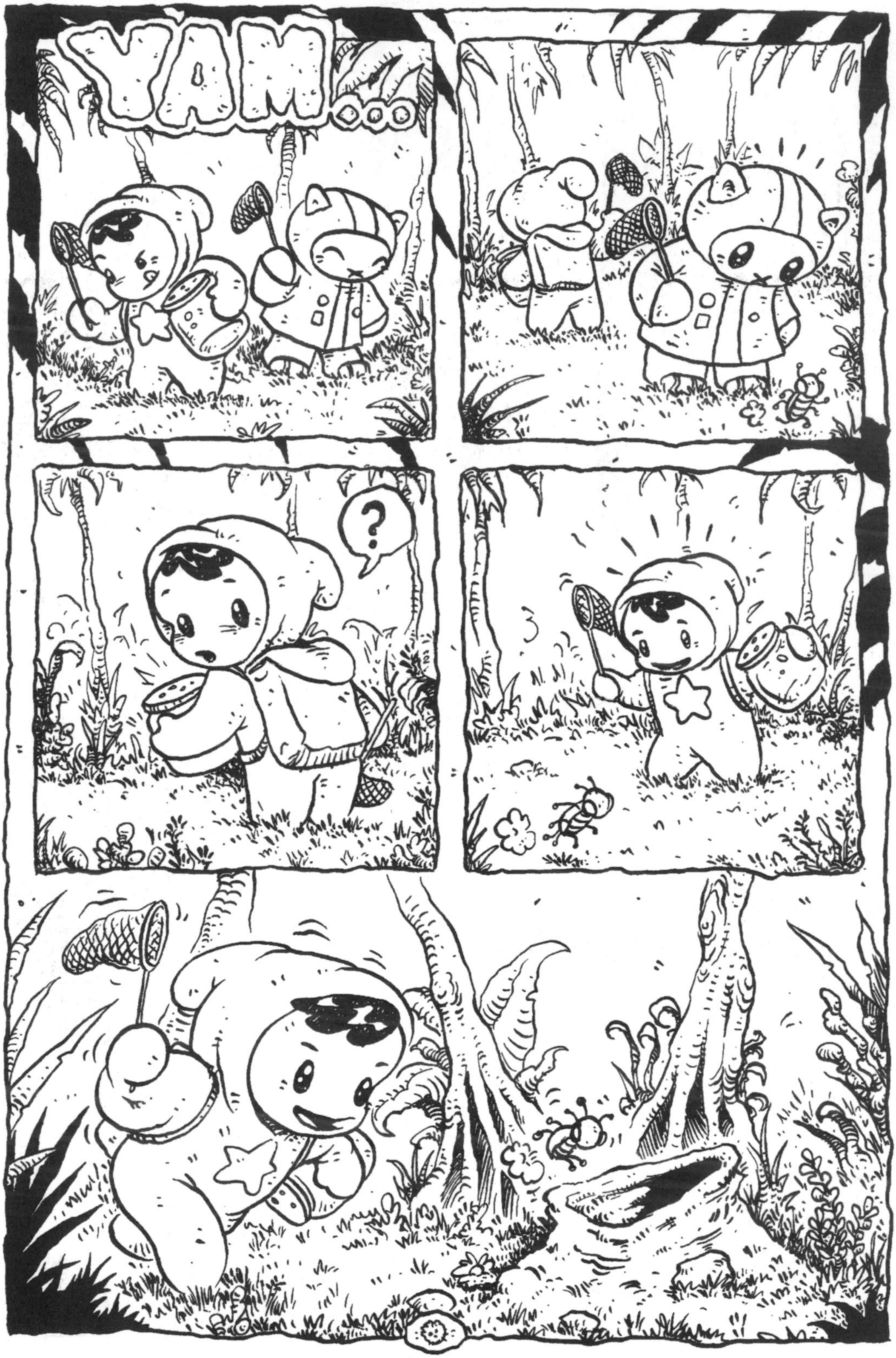
YAM...
?

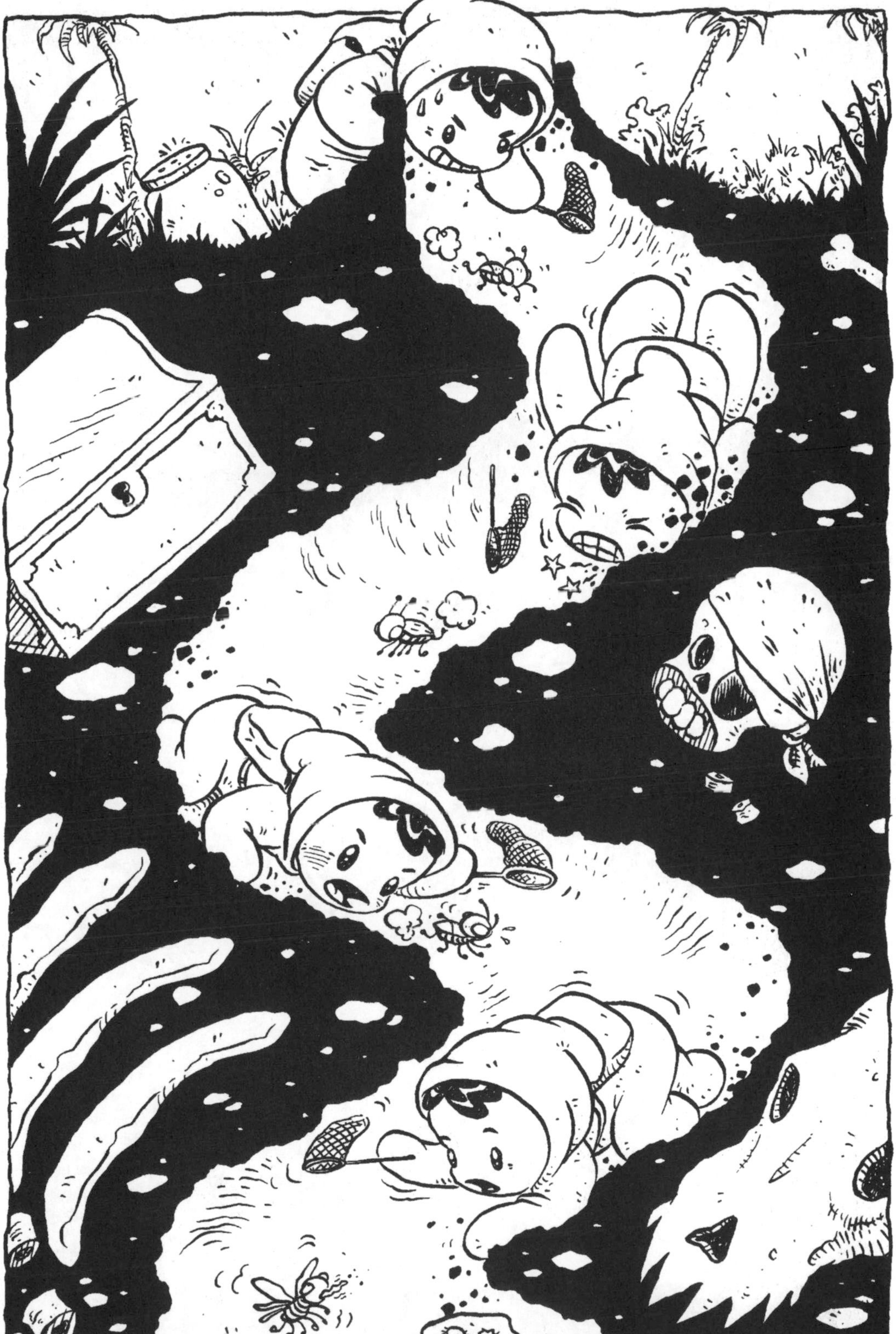

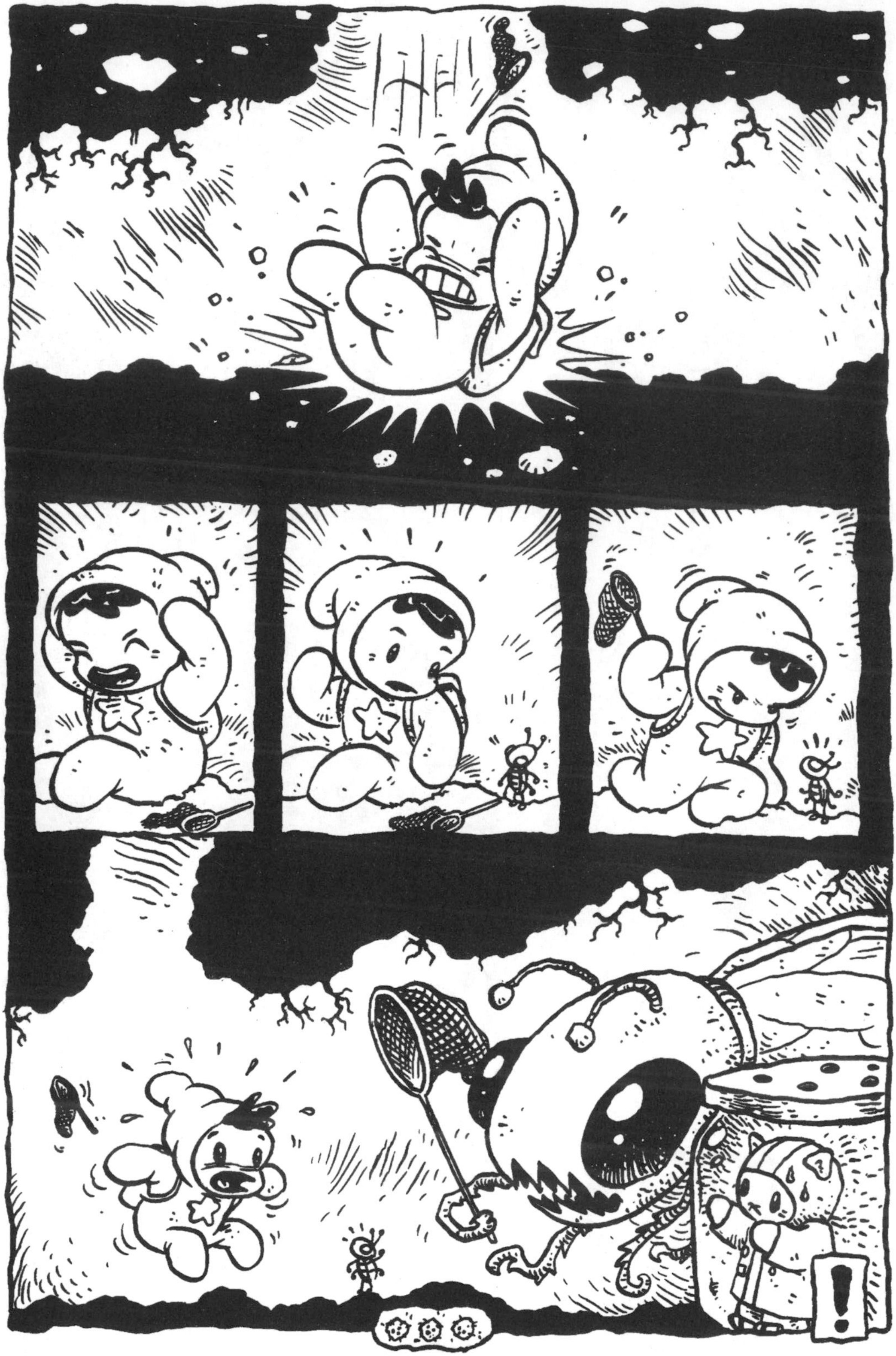

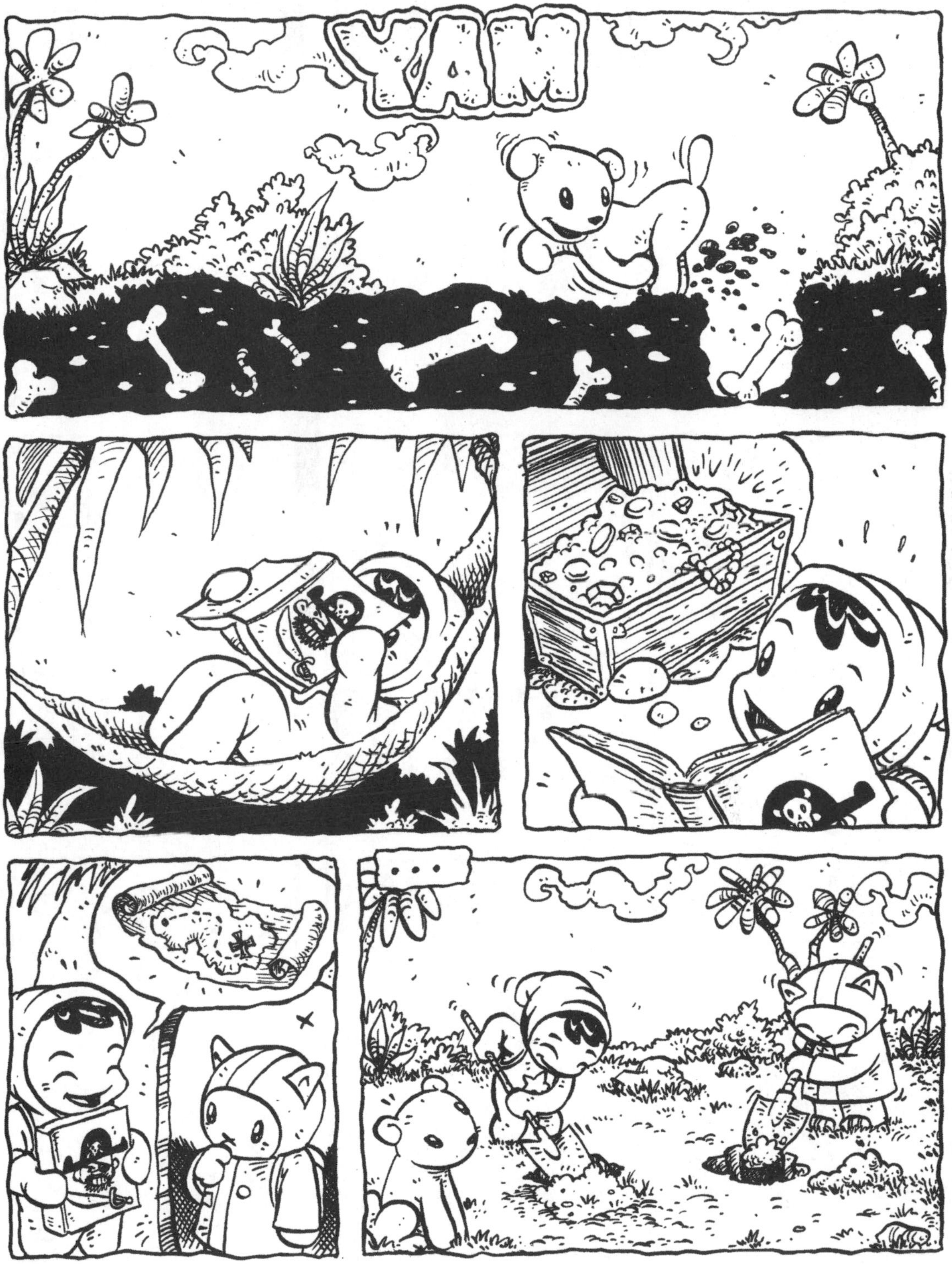
YAM
...

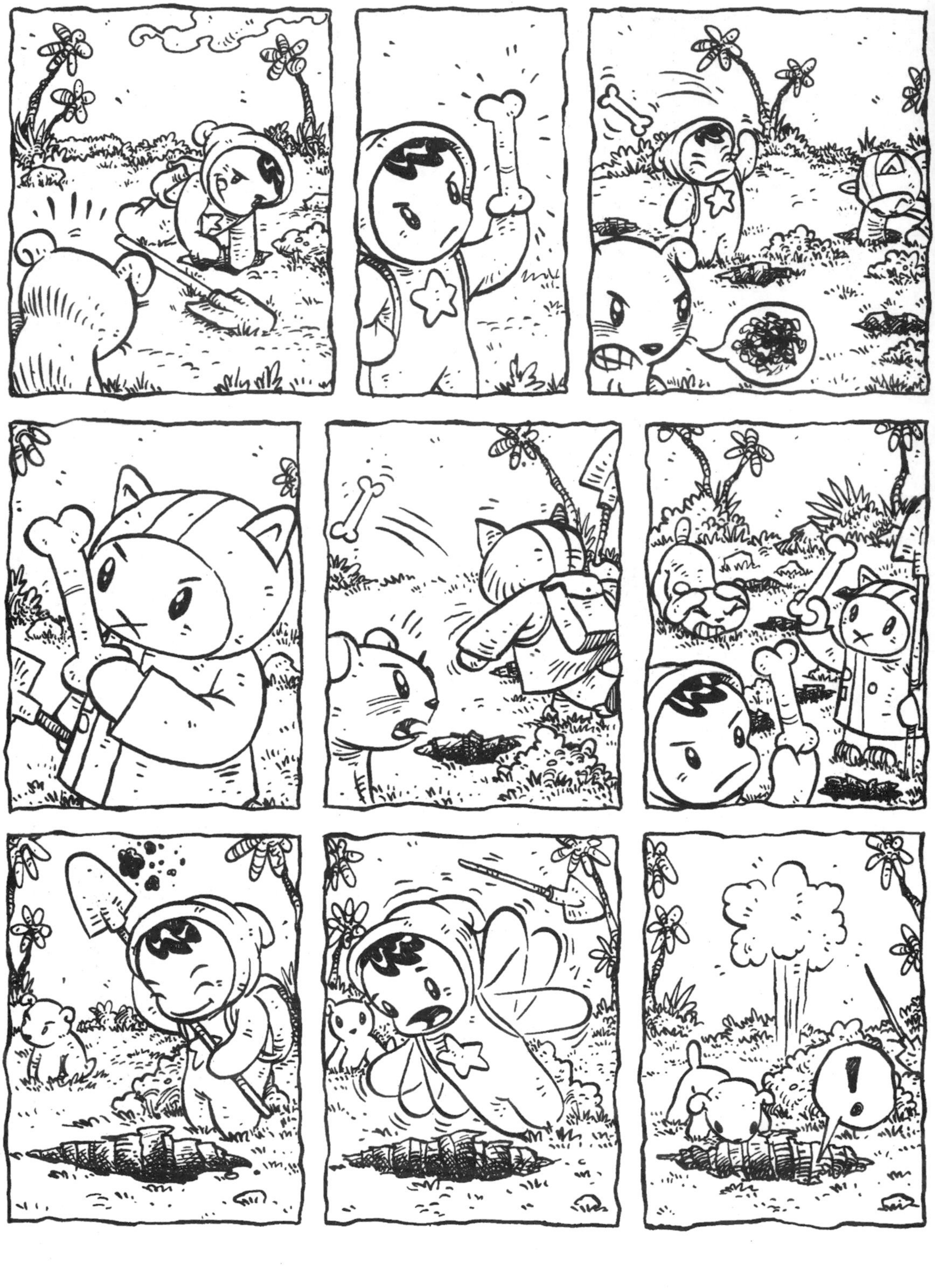
!

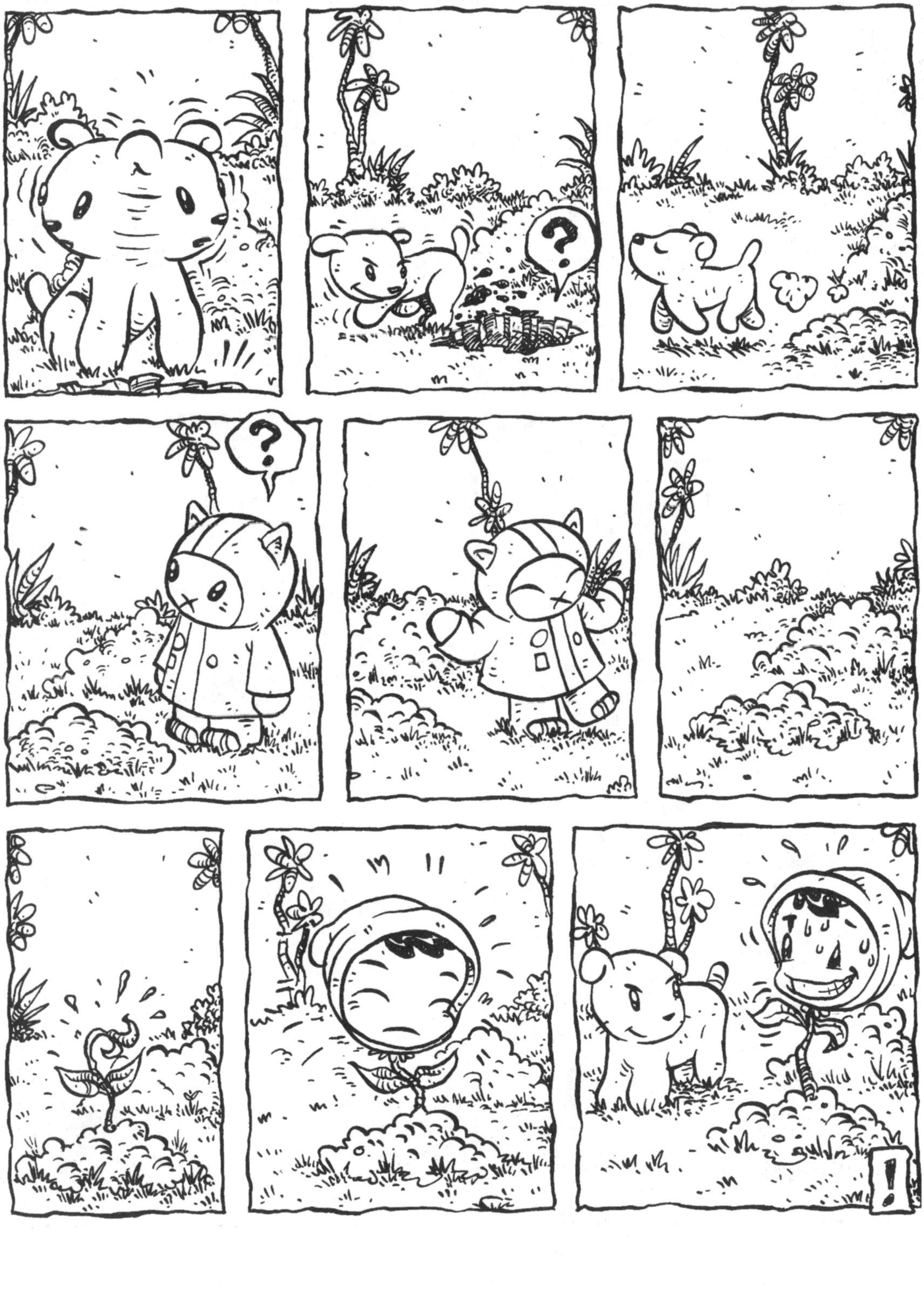
?
?
!

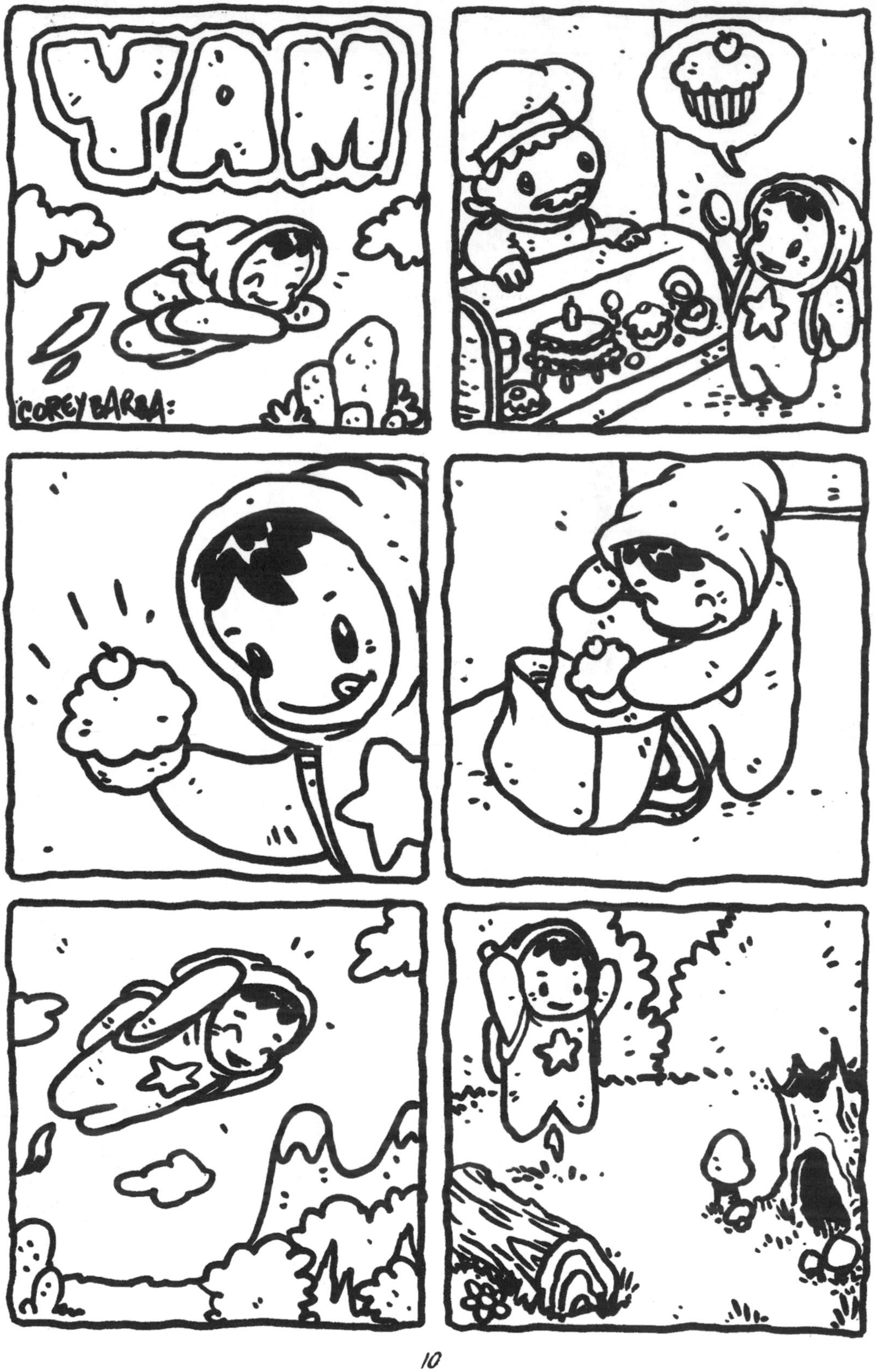
YAM
COREY BARBA

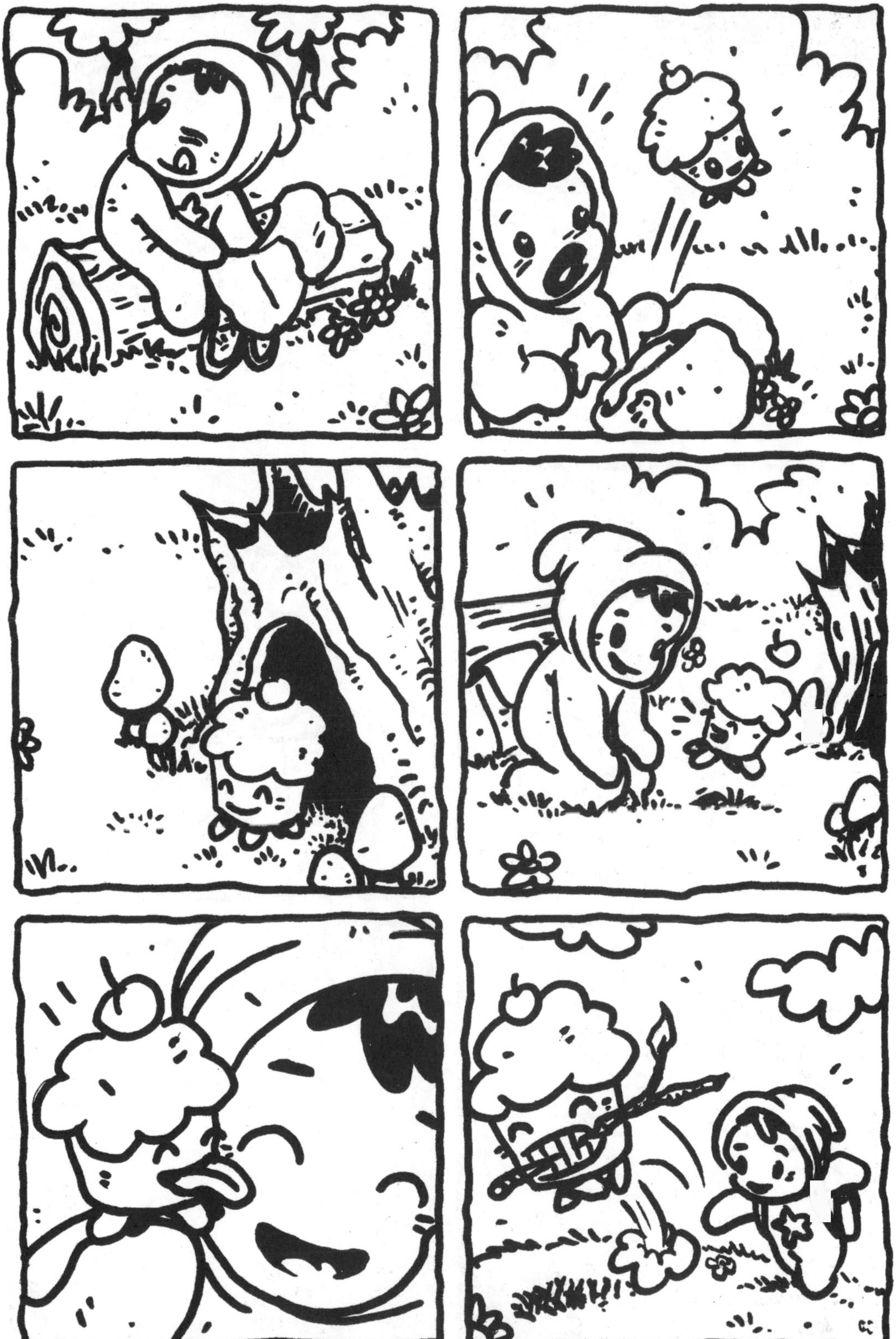

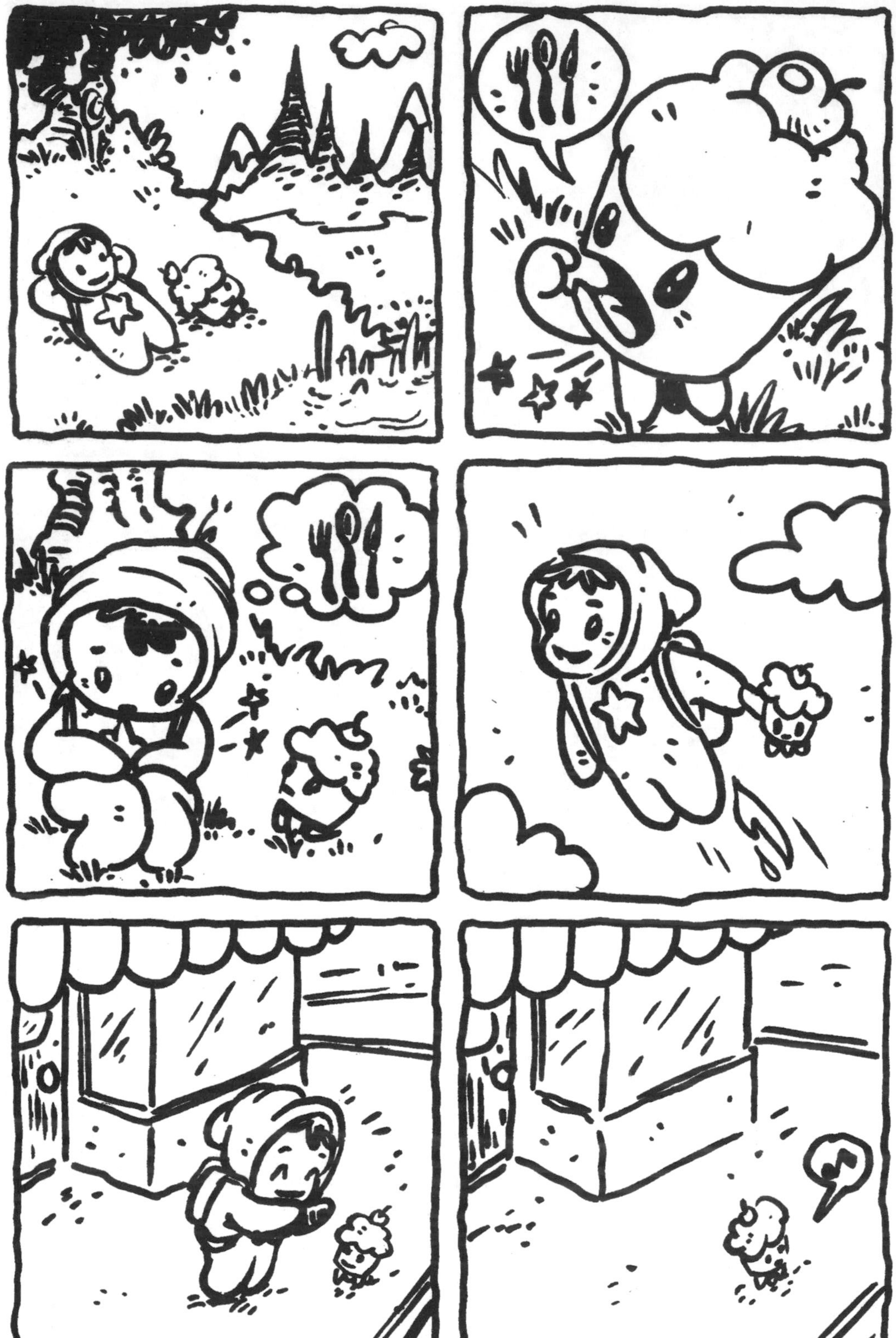

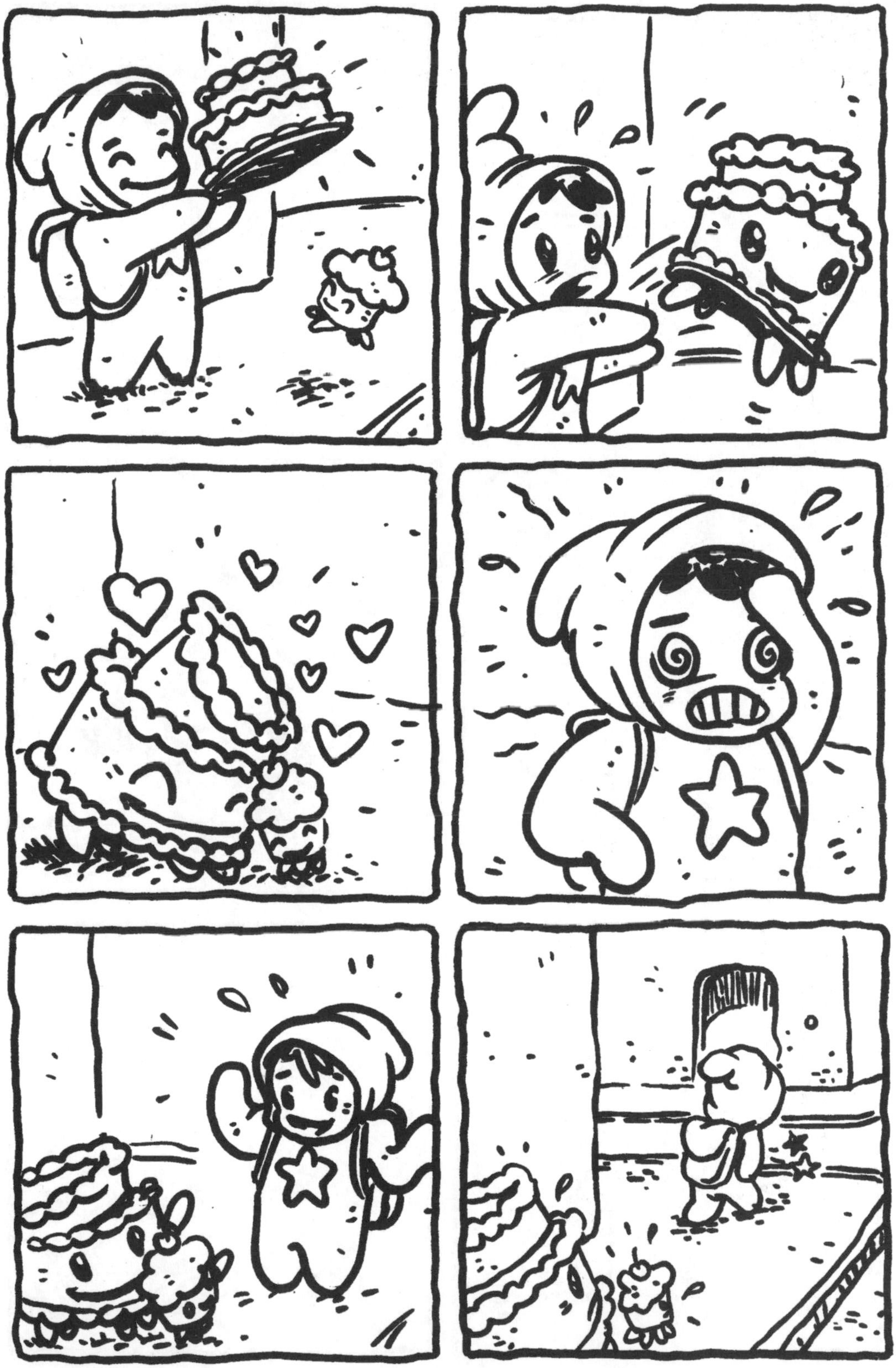

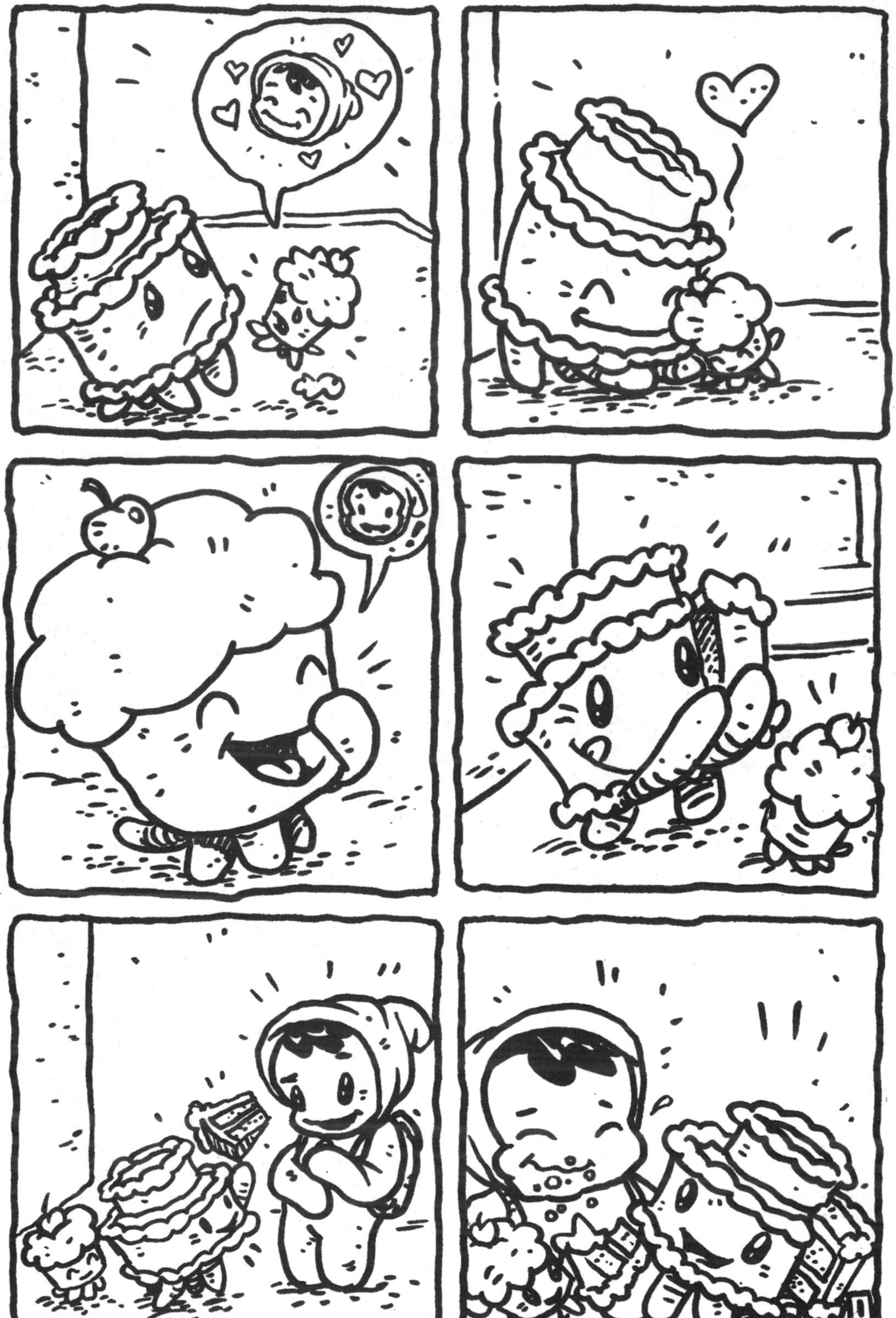
!

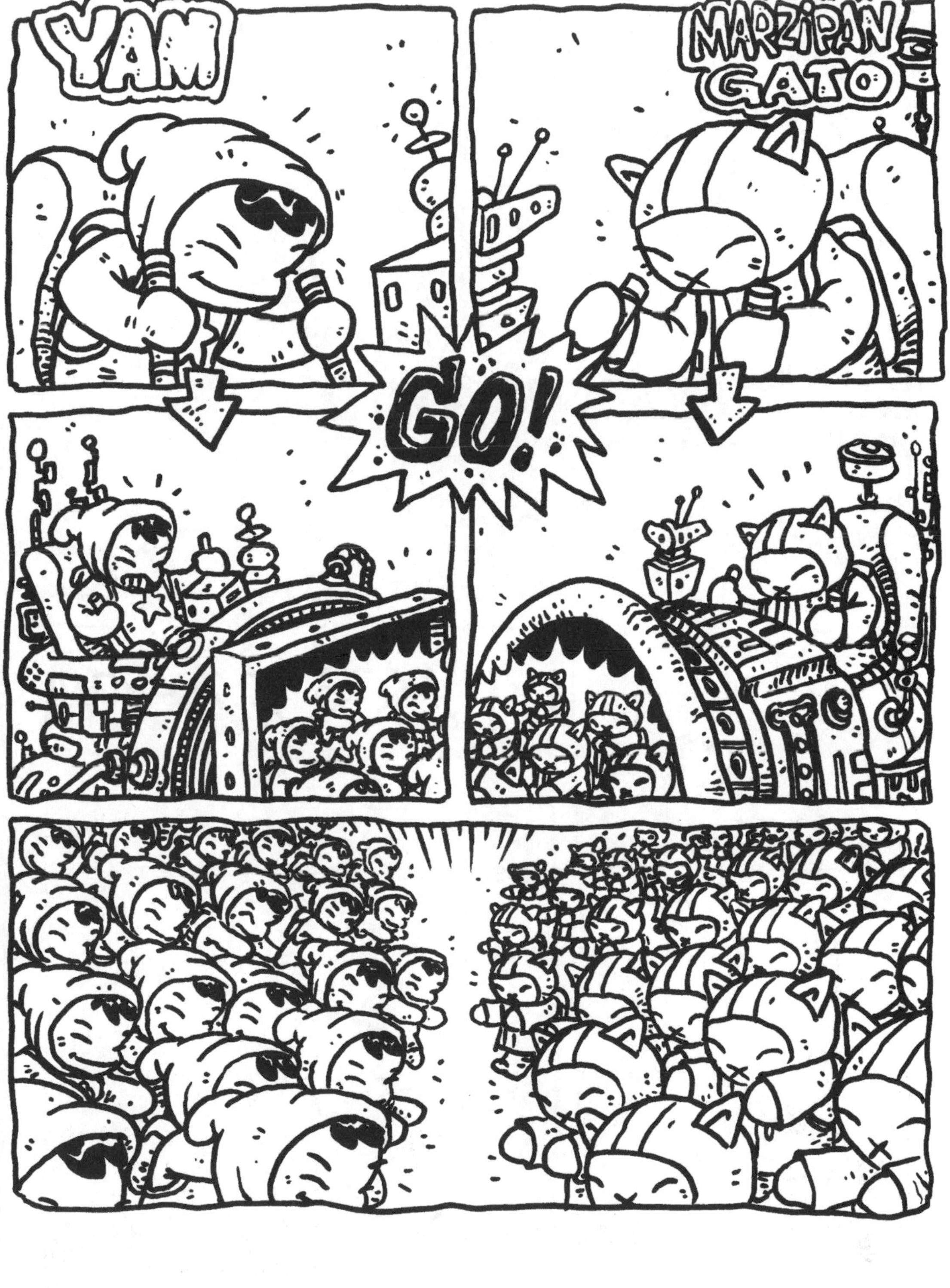
YAM
MARZIPAN GATO
GO!

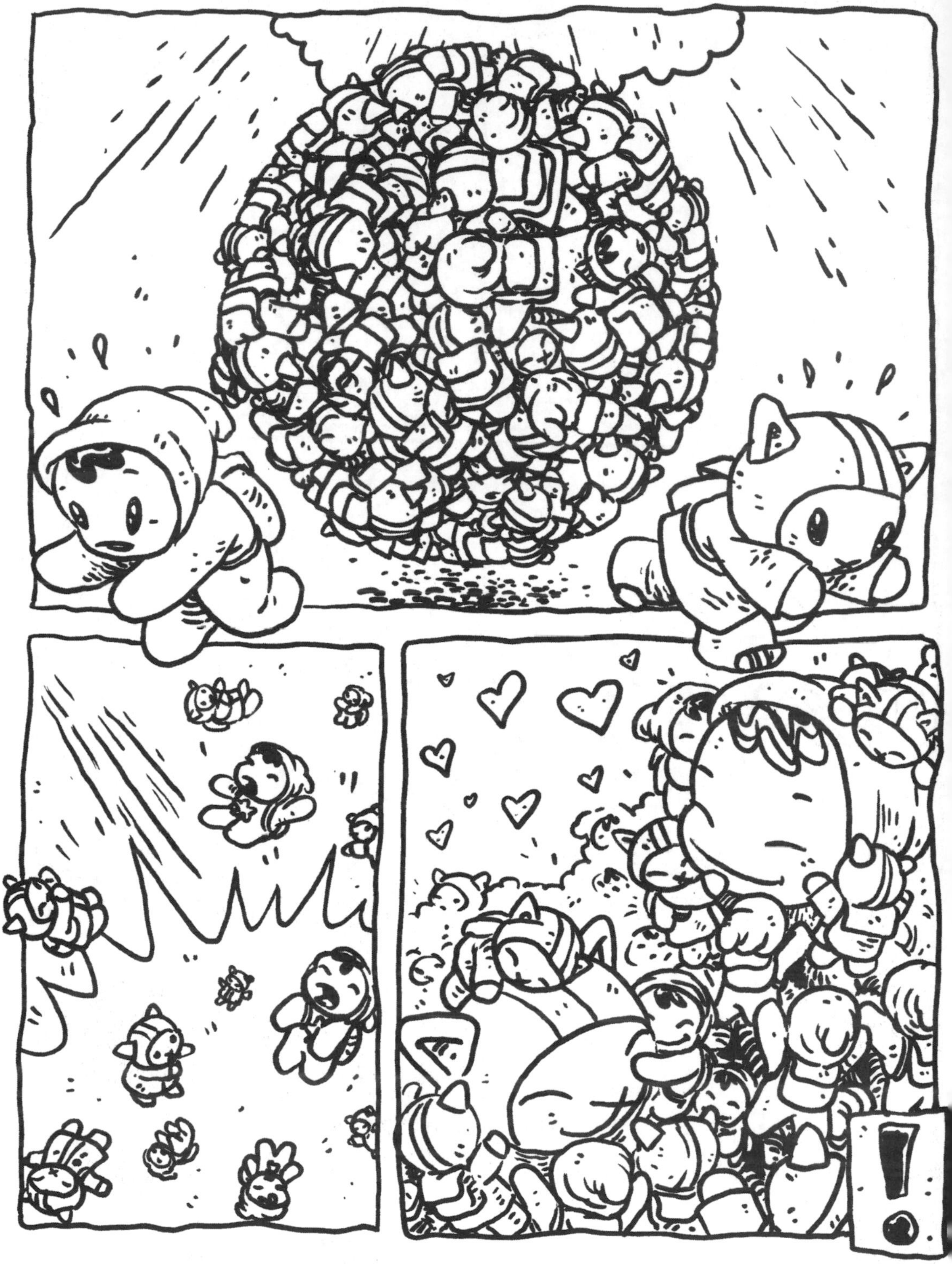
!

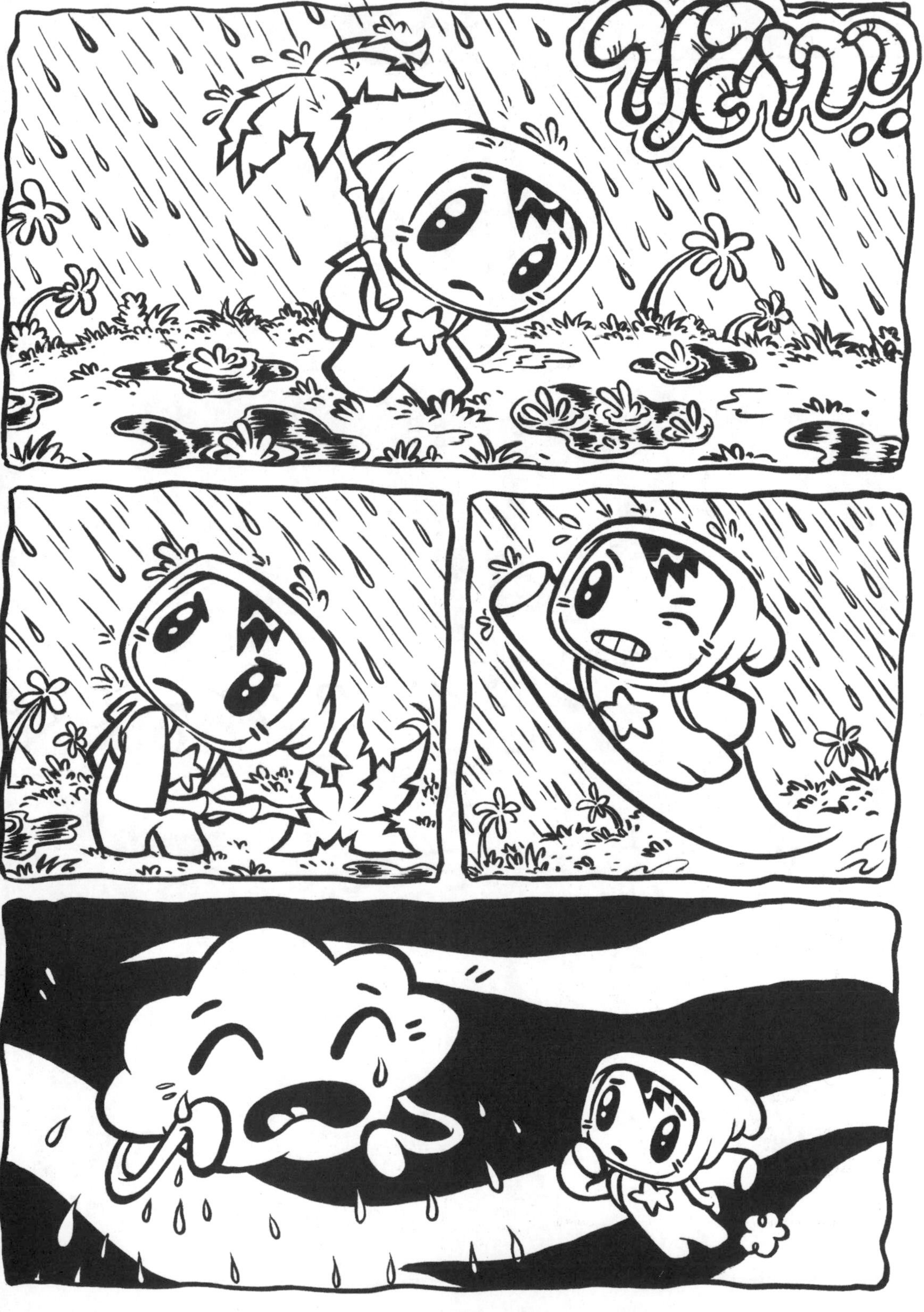

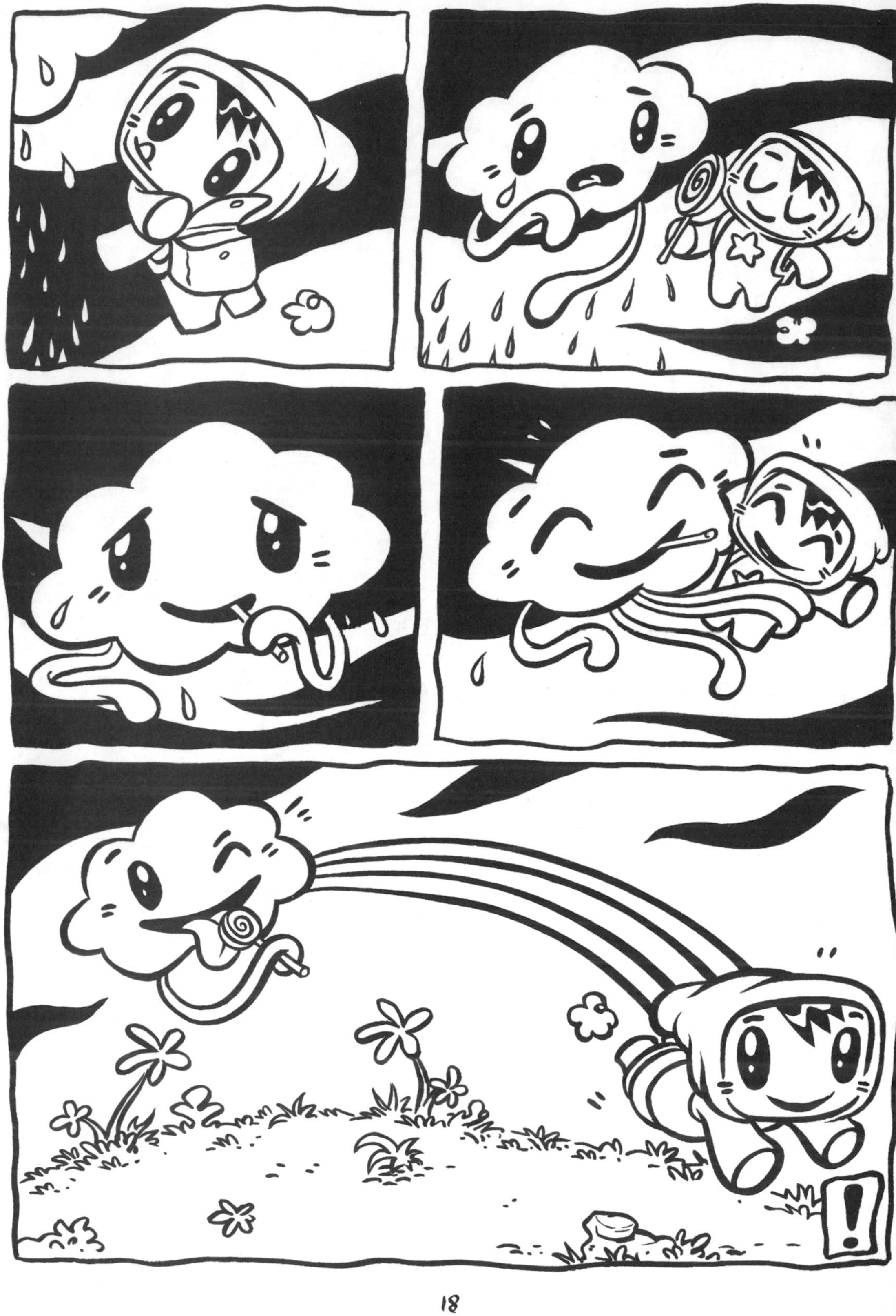
!

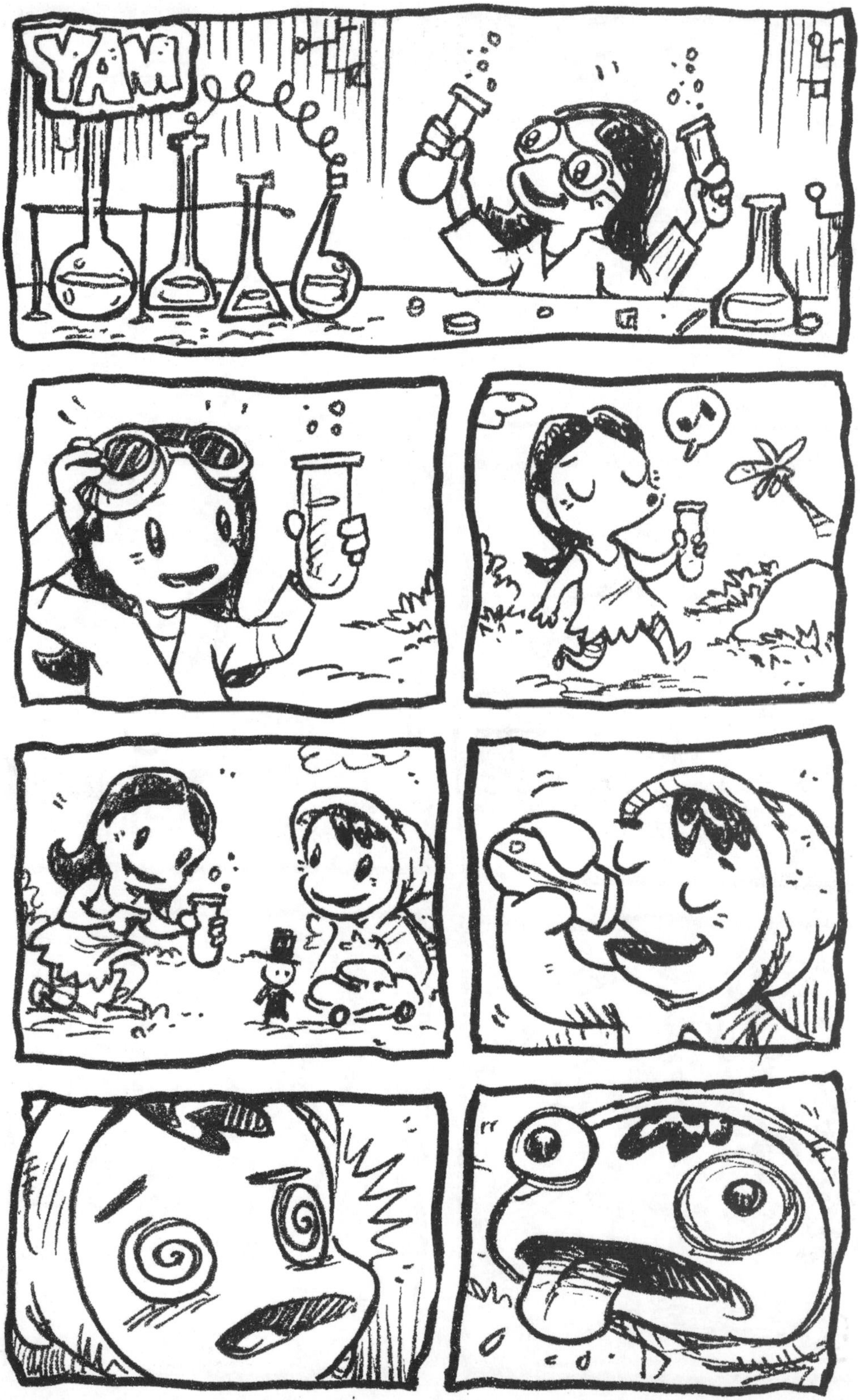
YAM

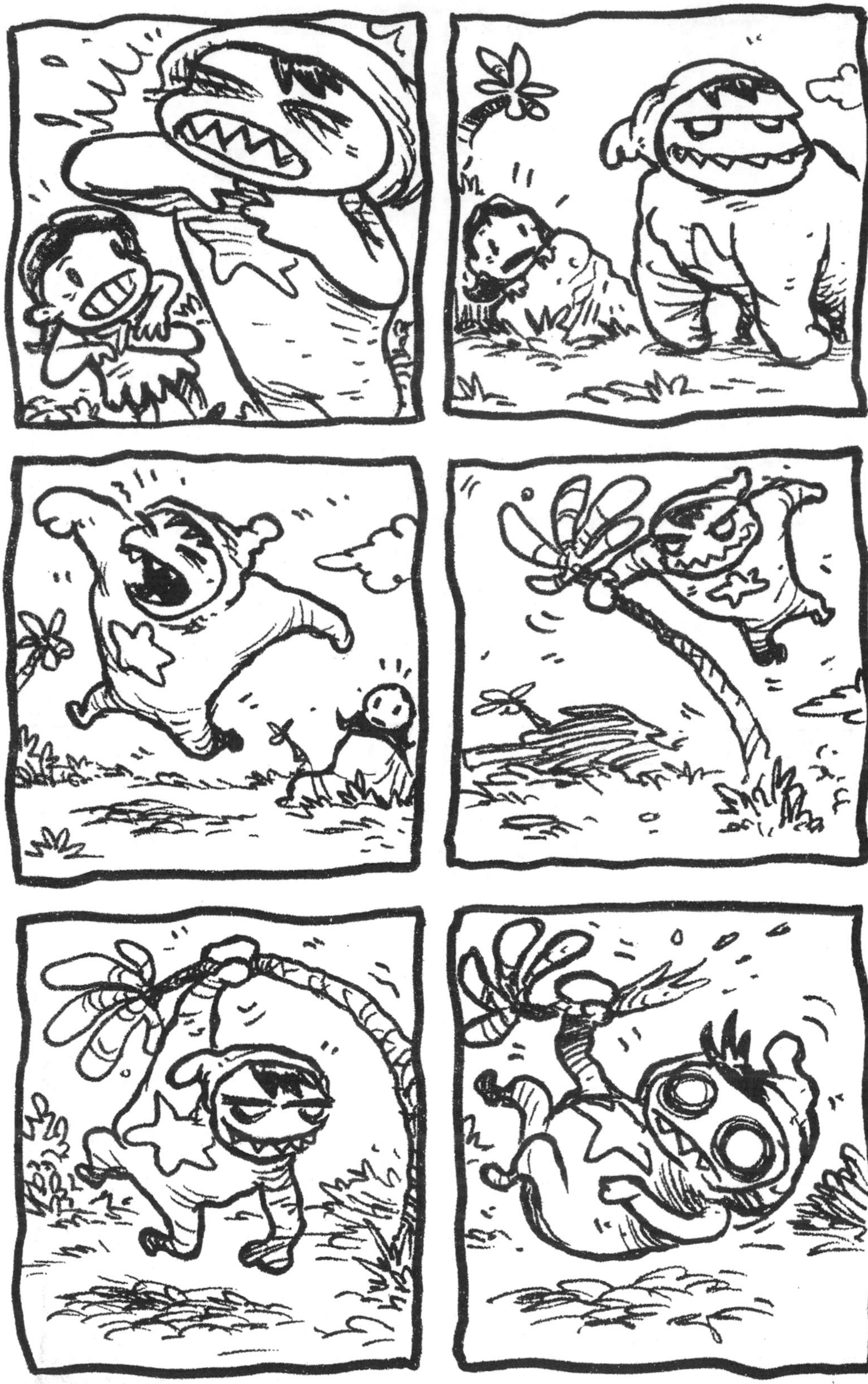

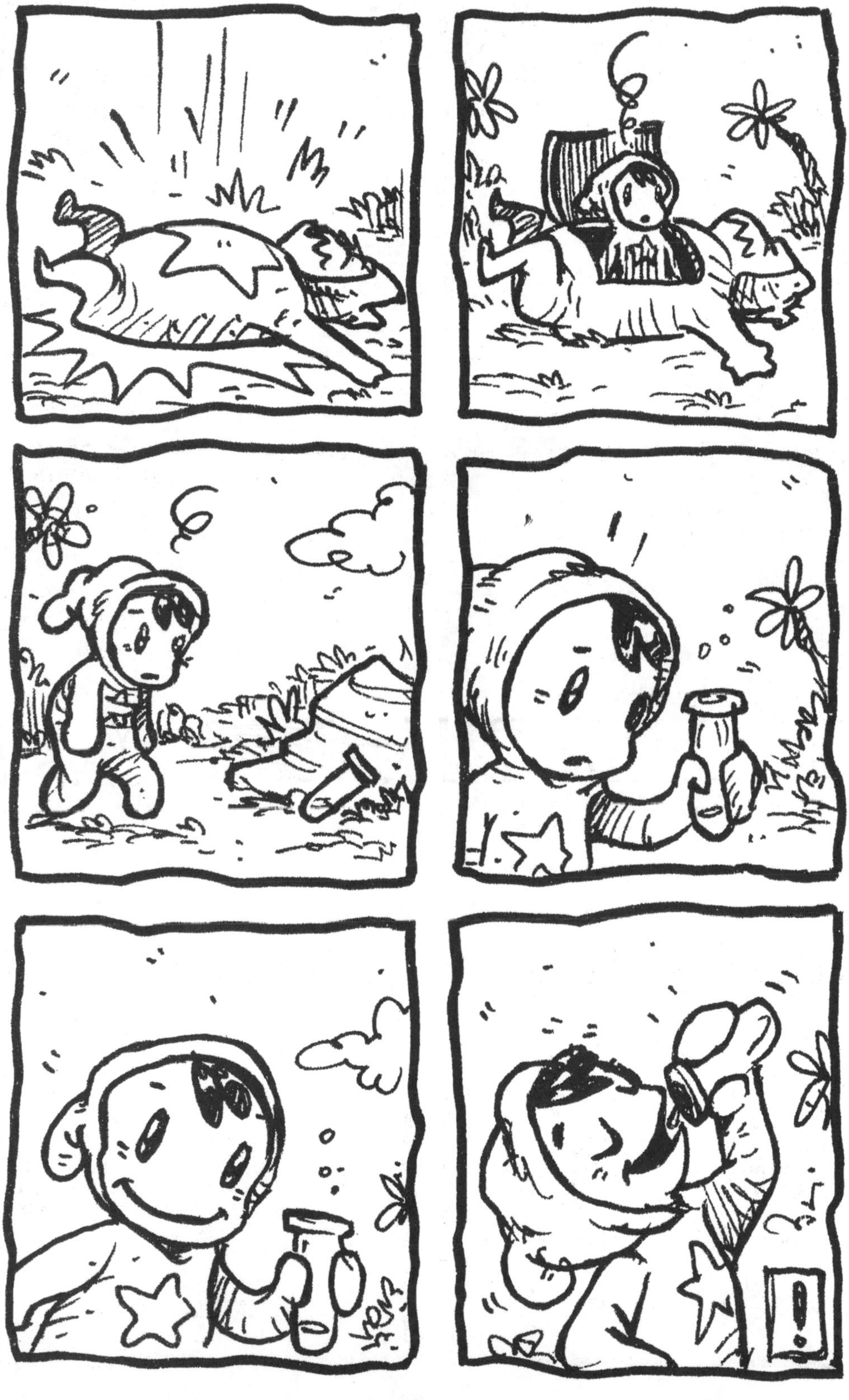

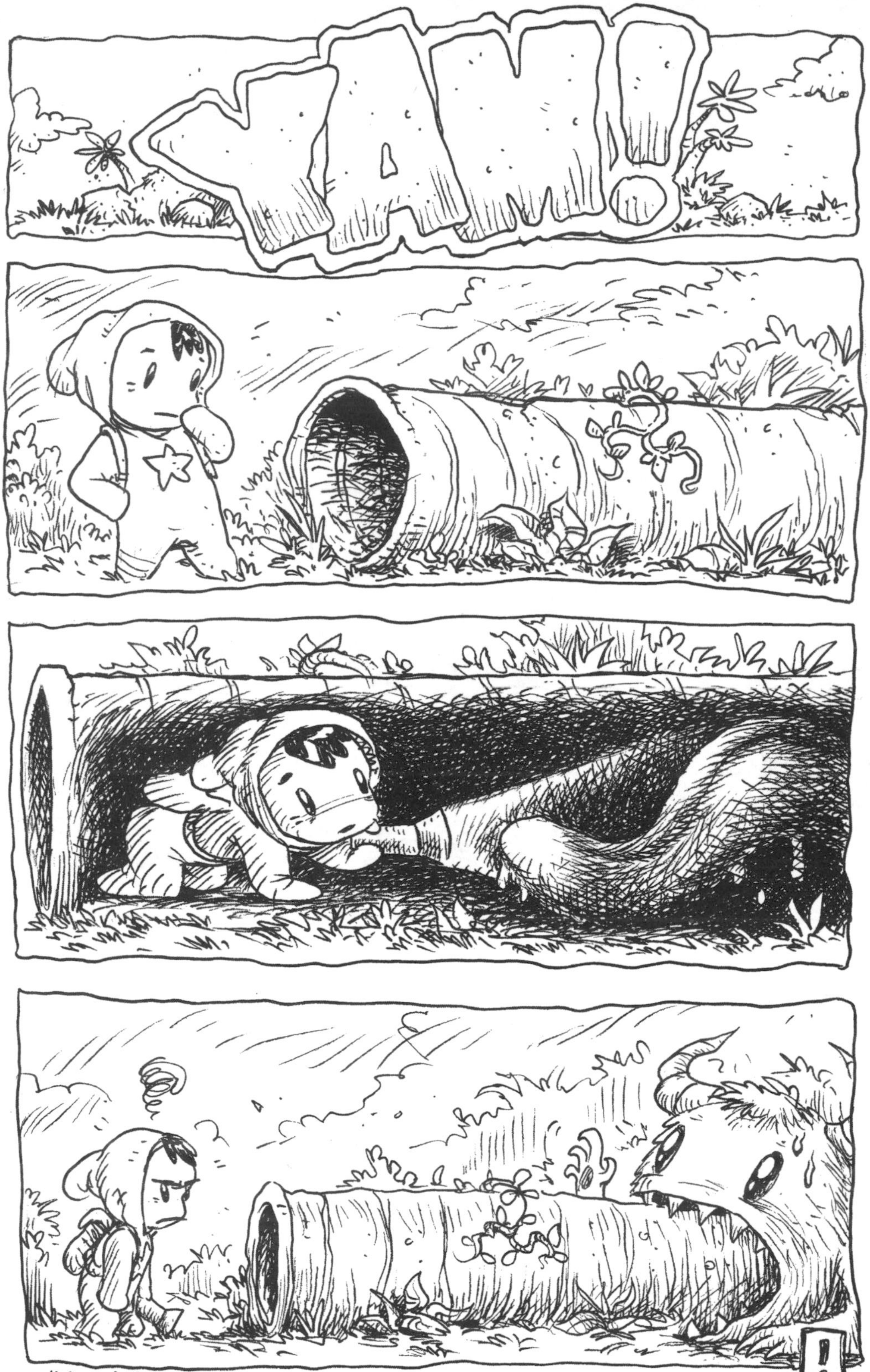
YAM!
!
COREY BARBA

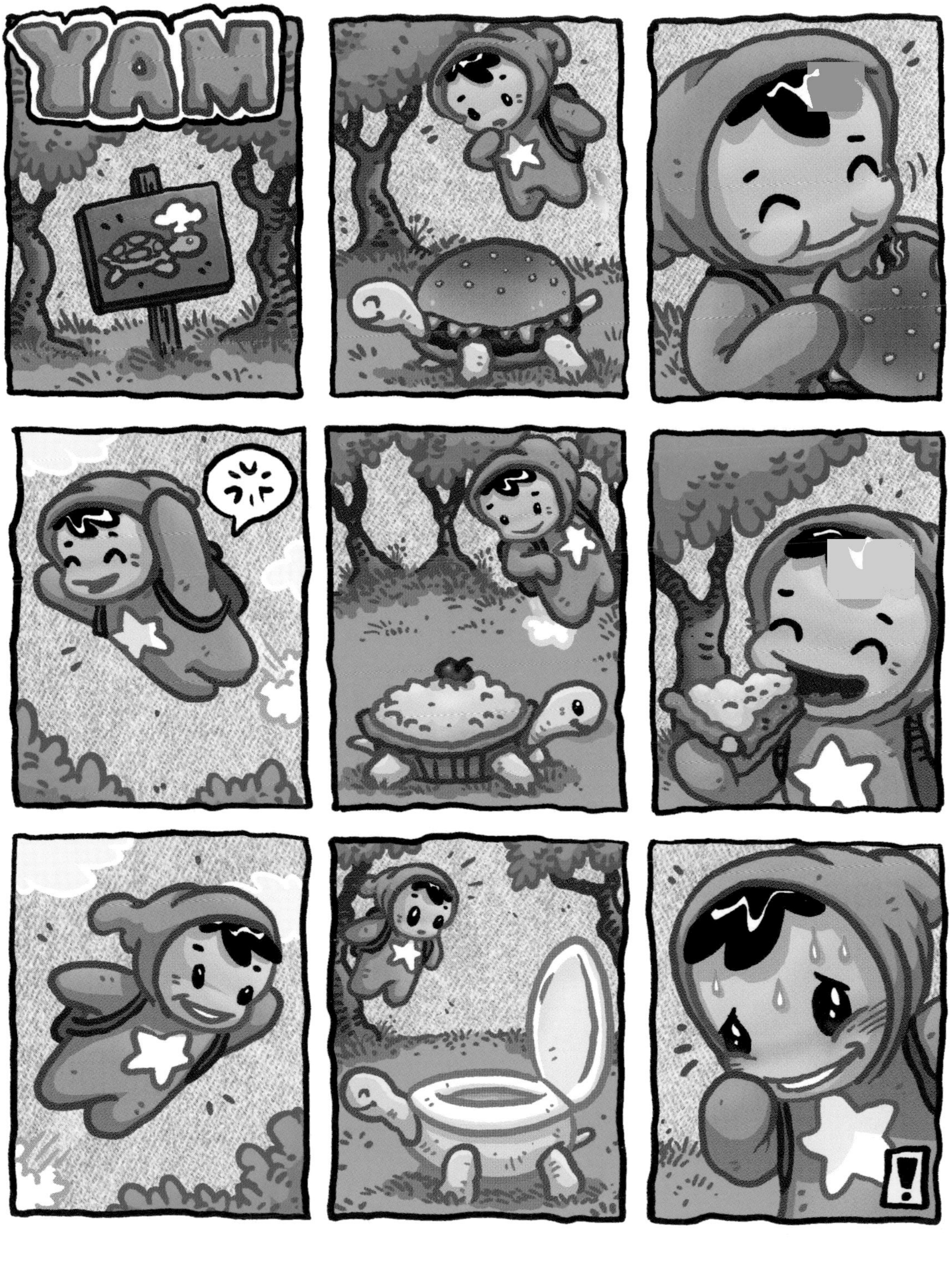
YAM
!

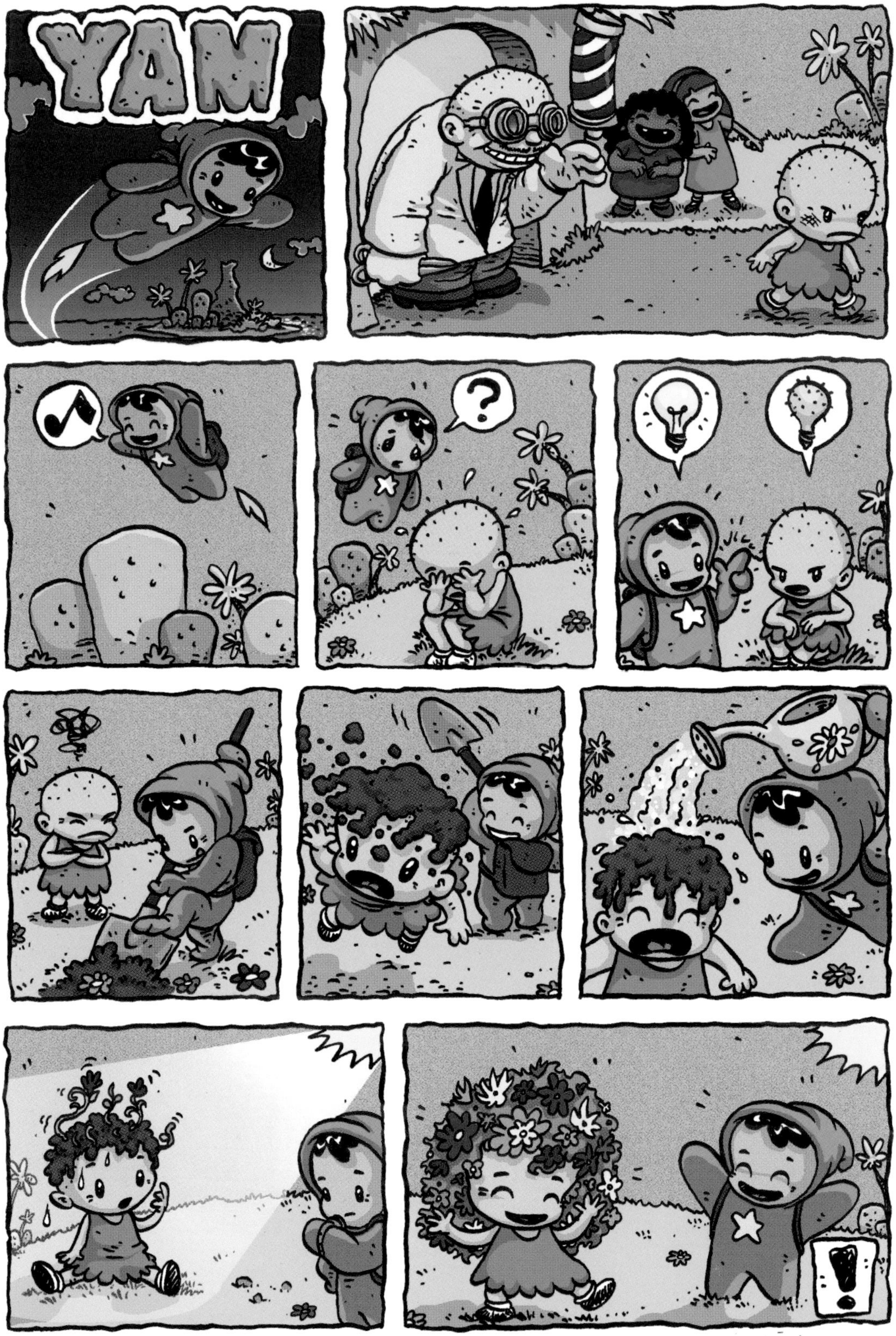
YAM

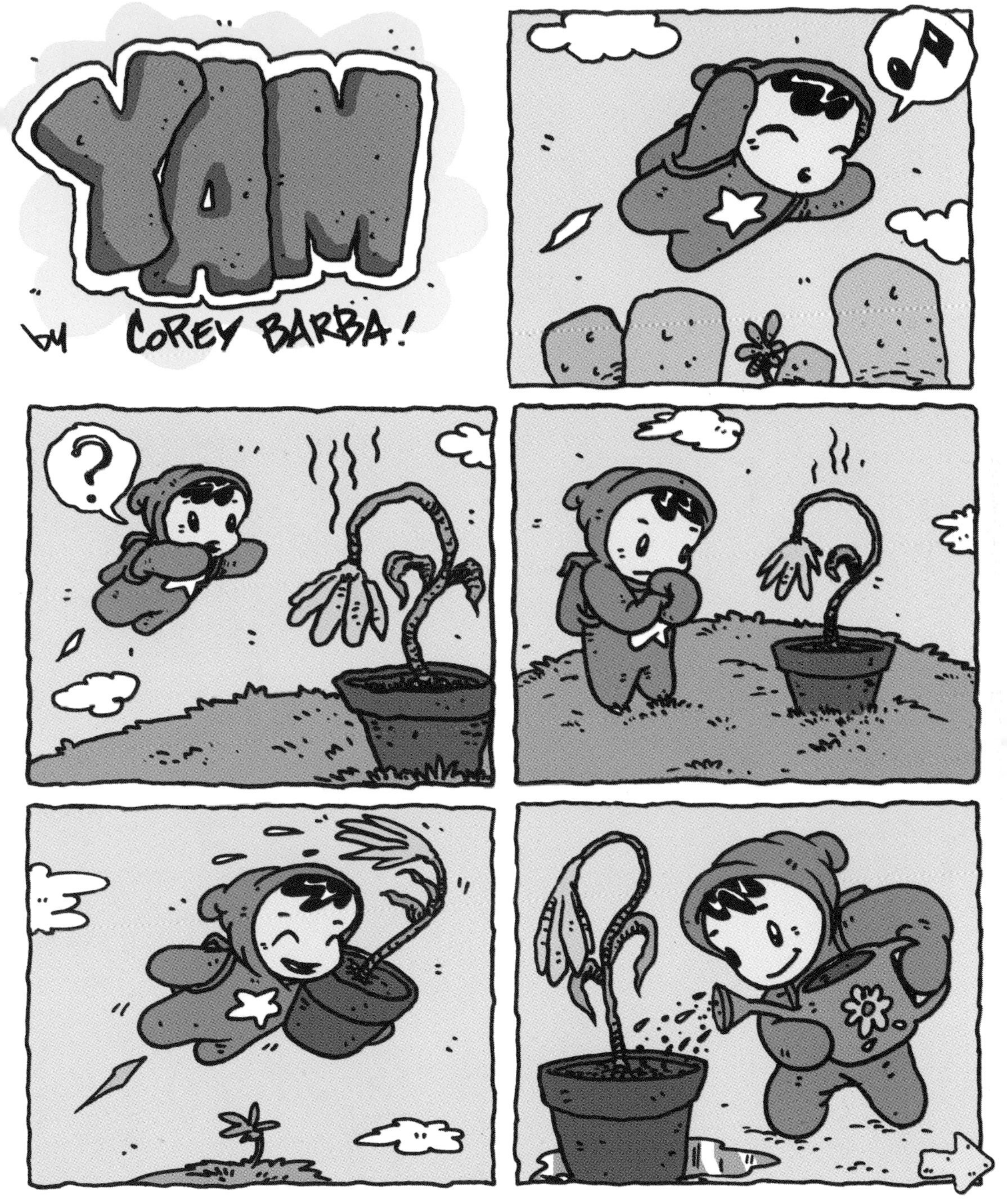
YAM
by COREY BARBA!
?

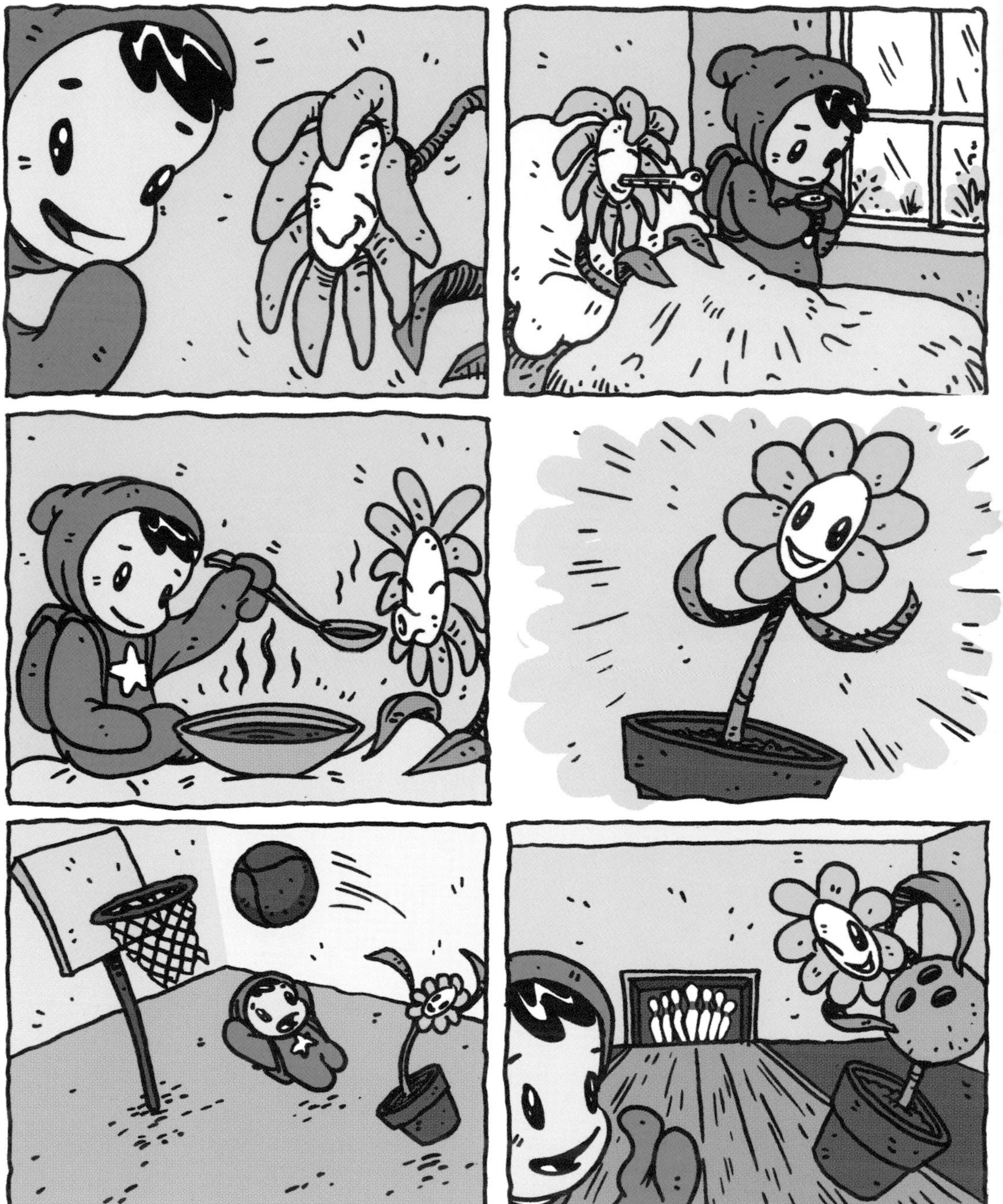

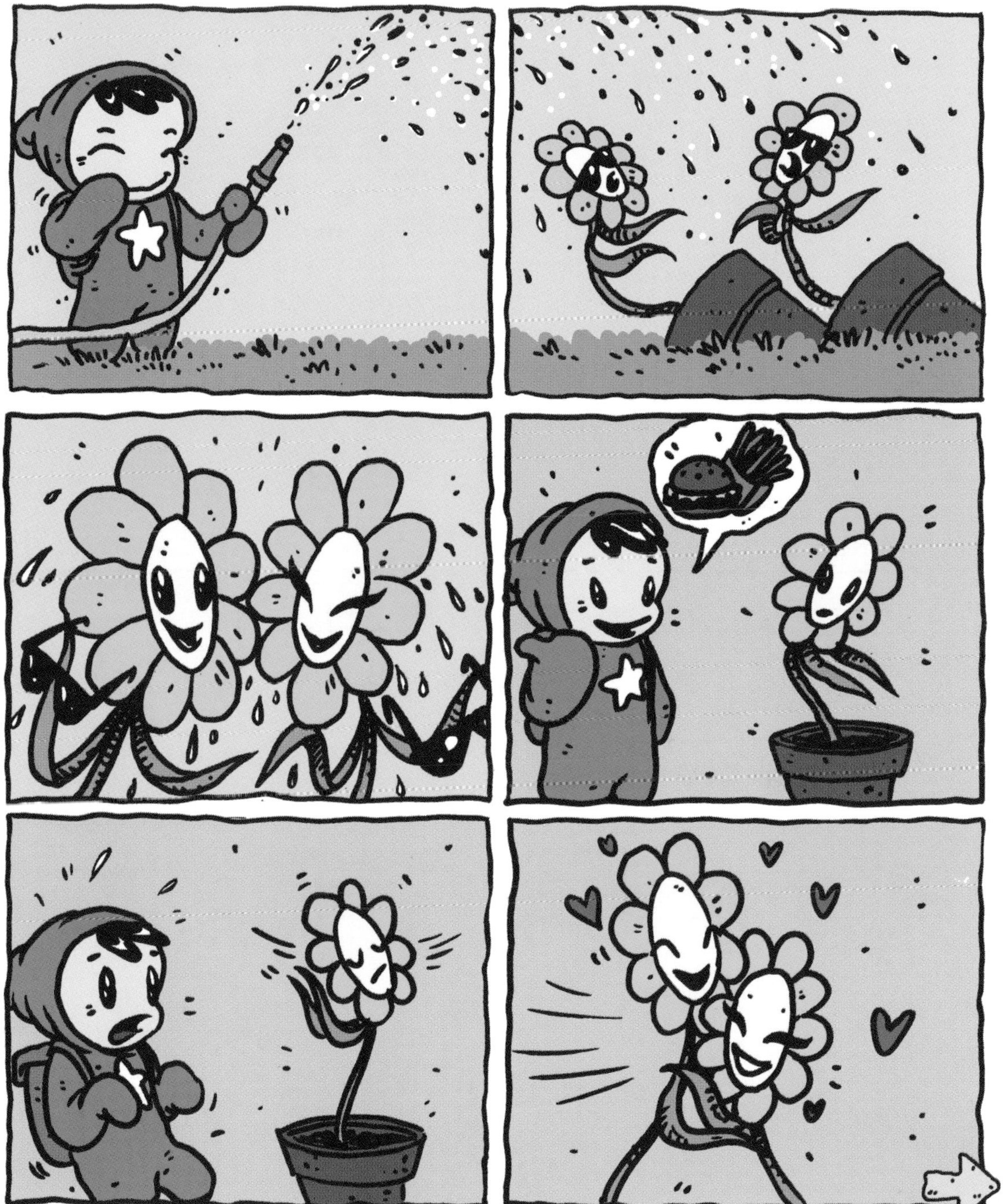

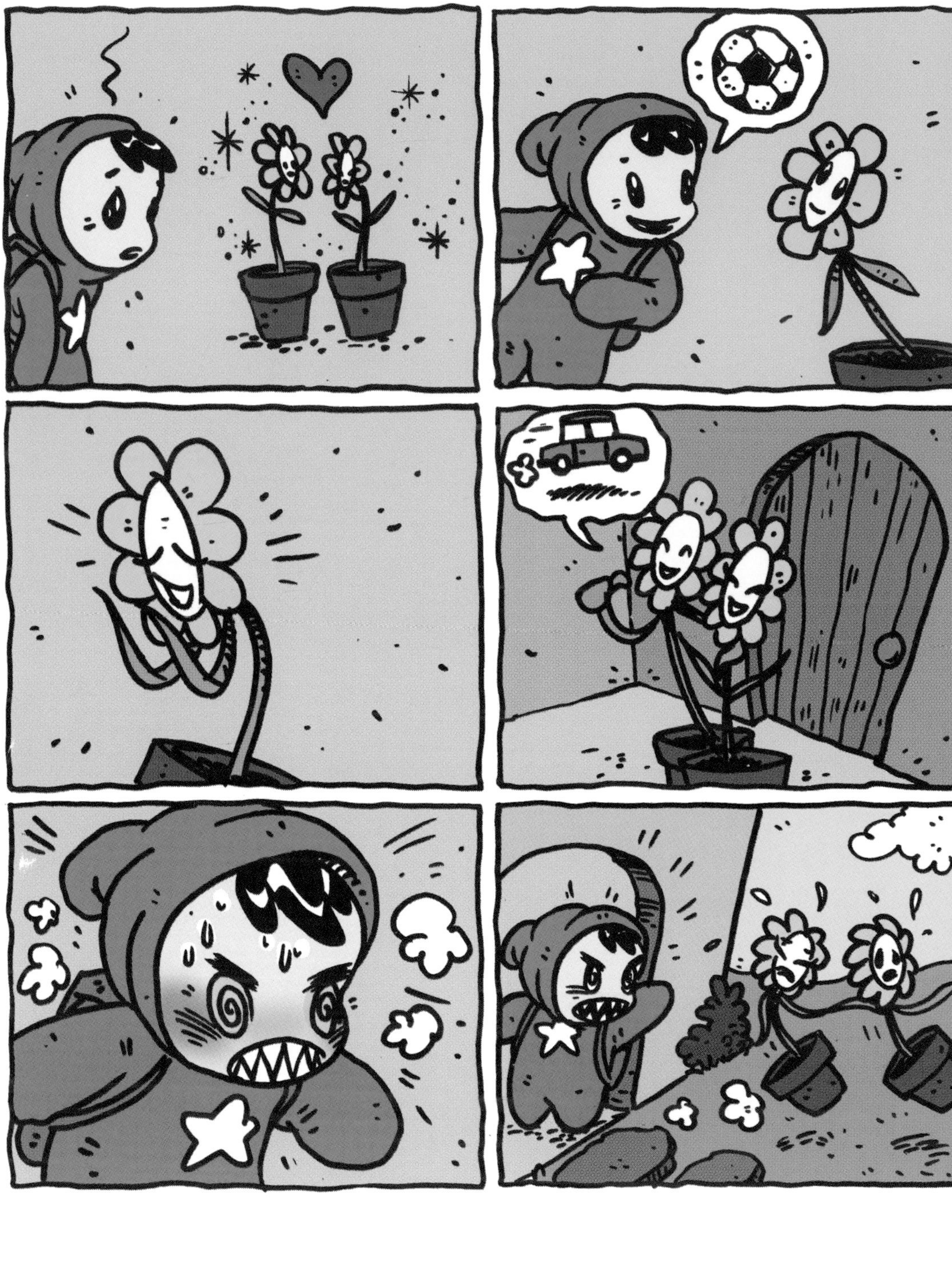

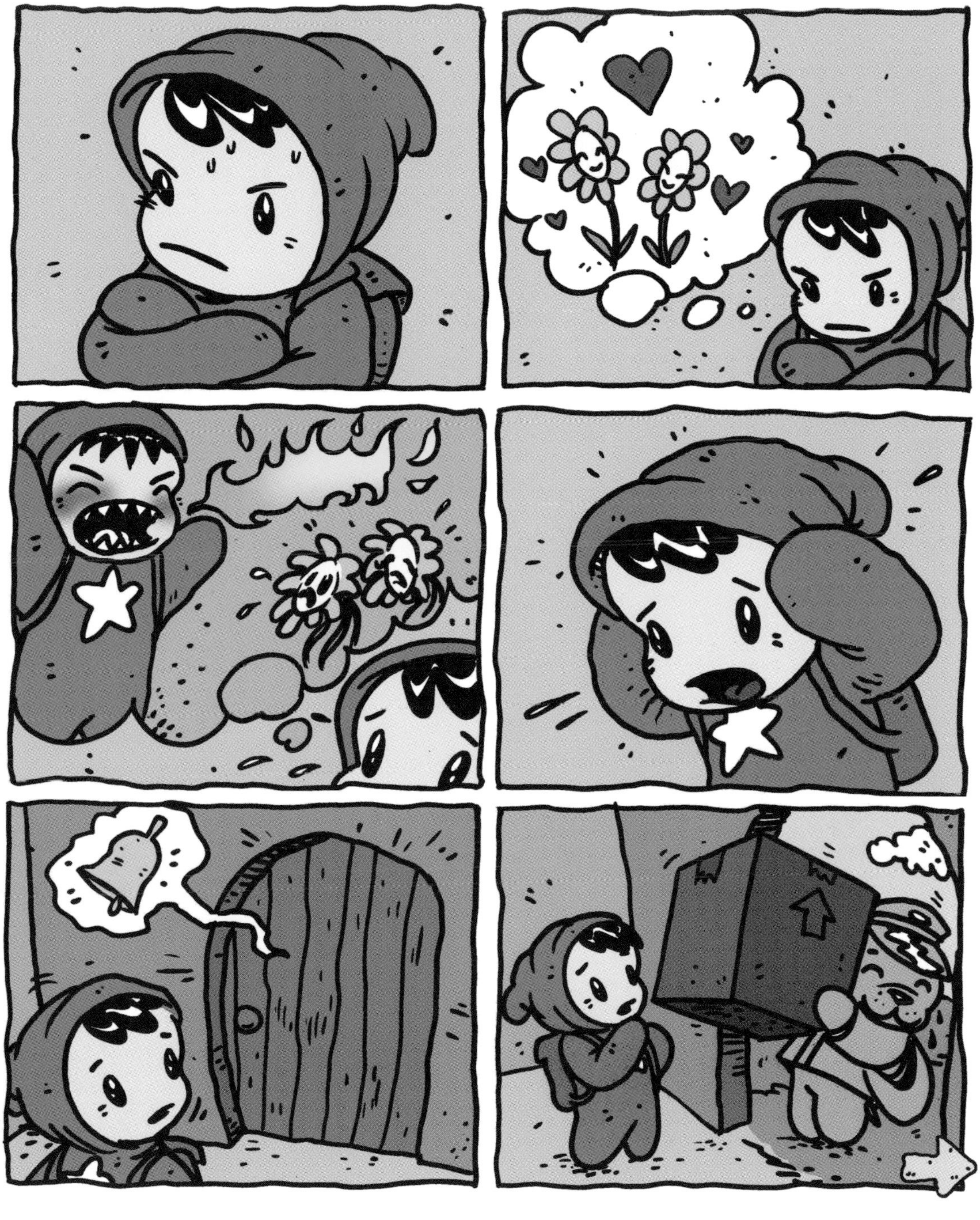

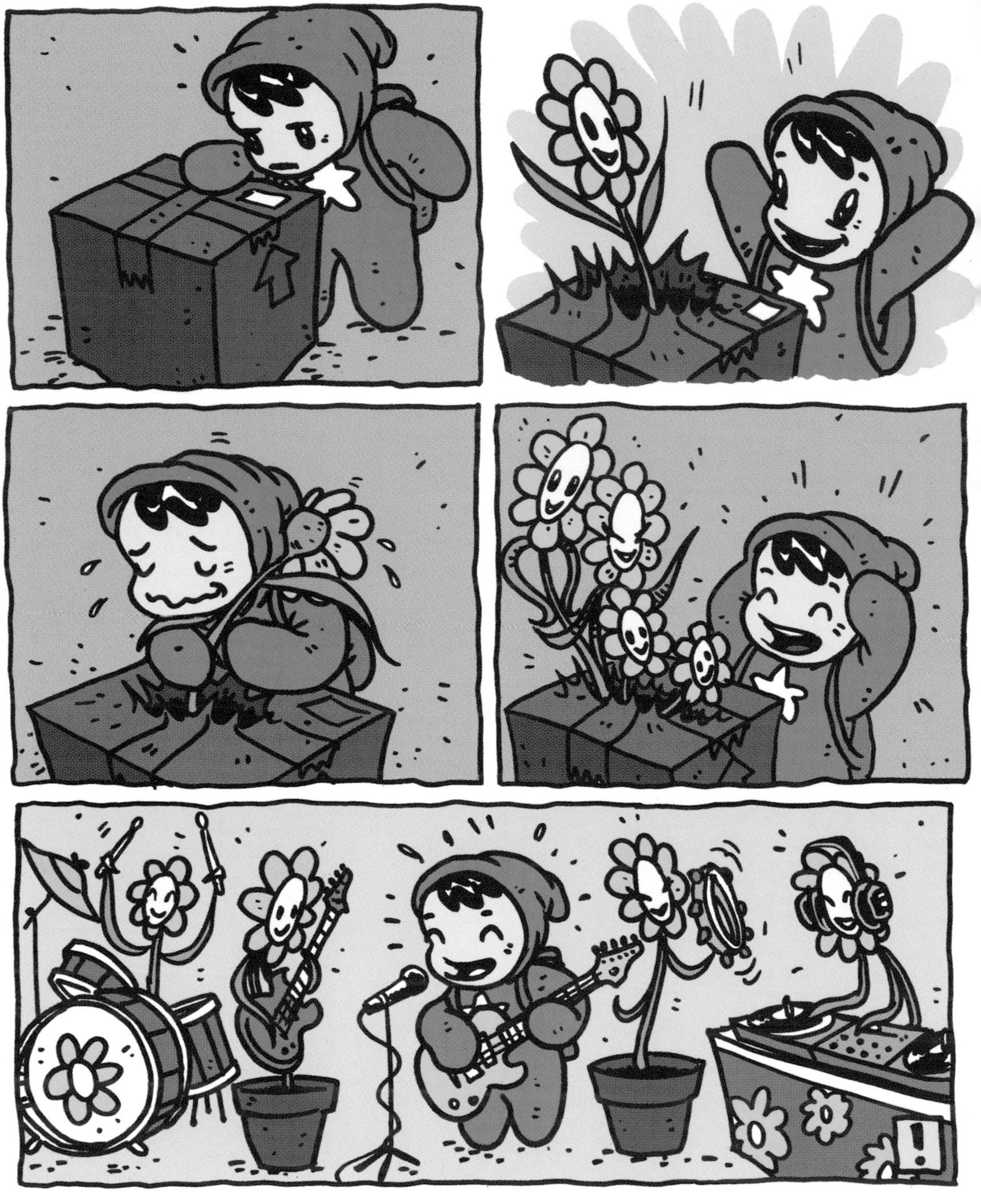

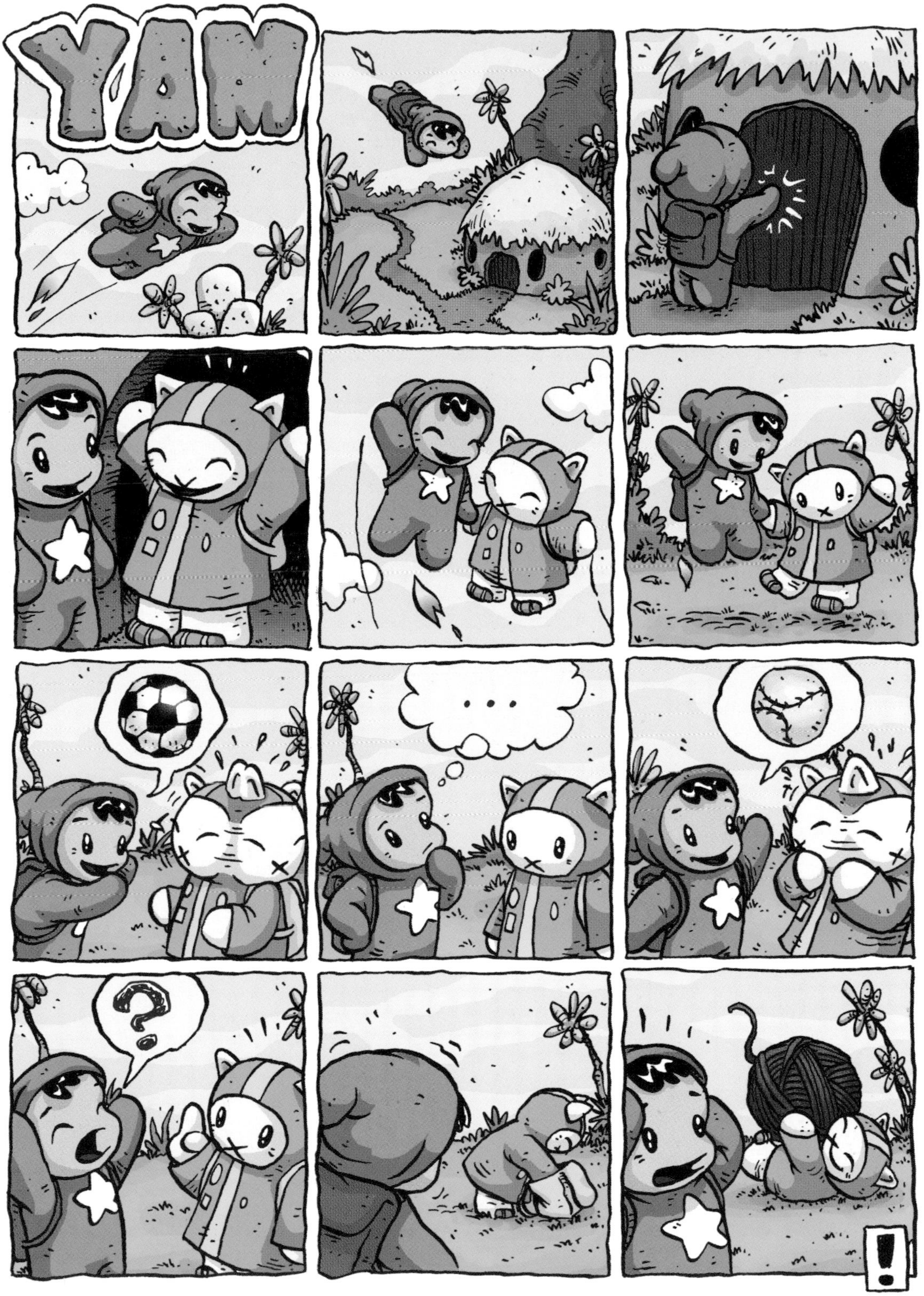
YAM
...
?
!

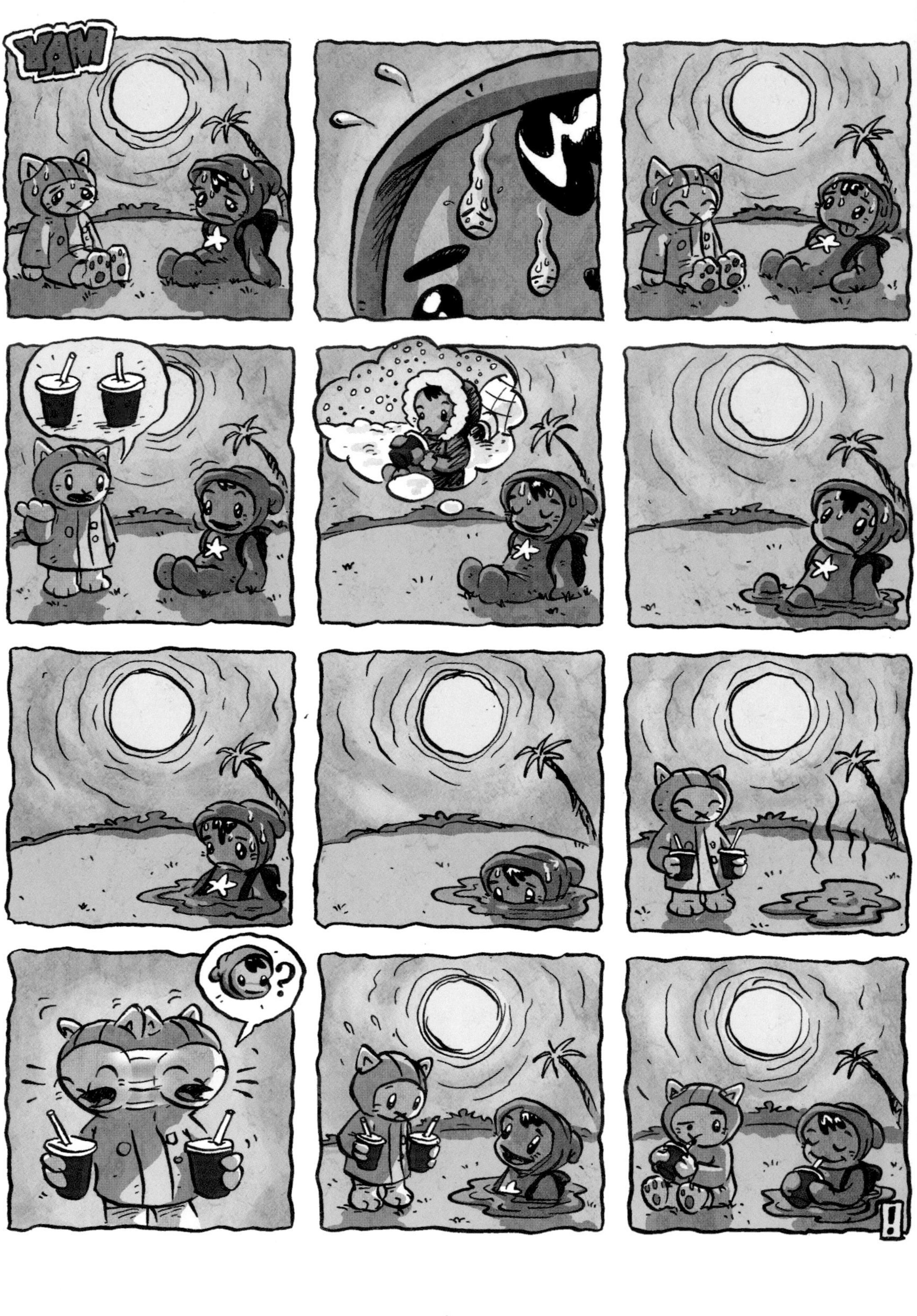
YAM
?
!

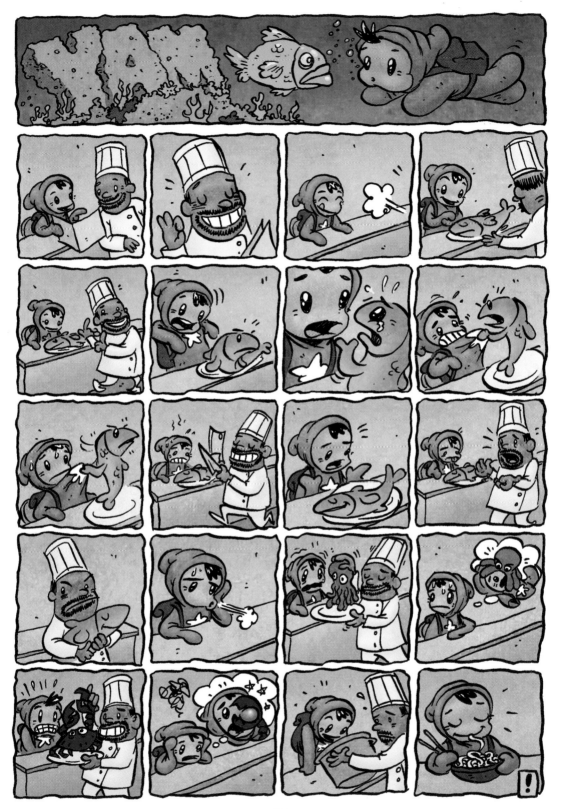

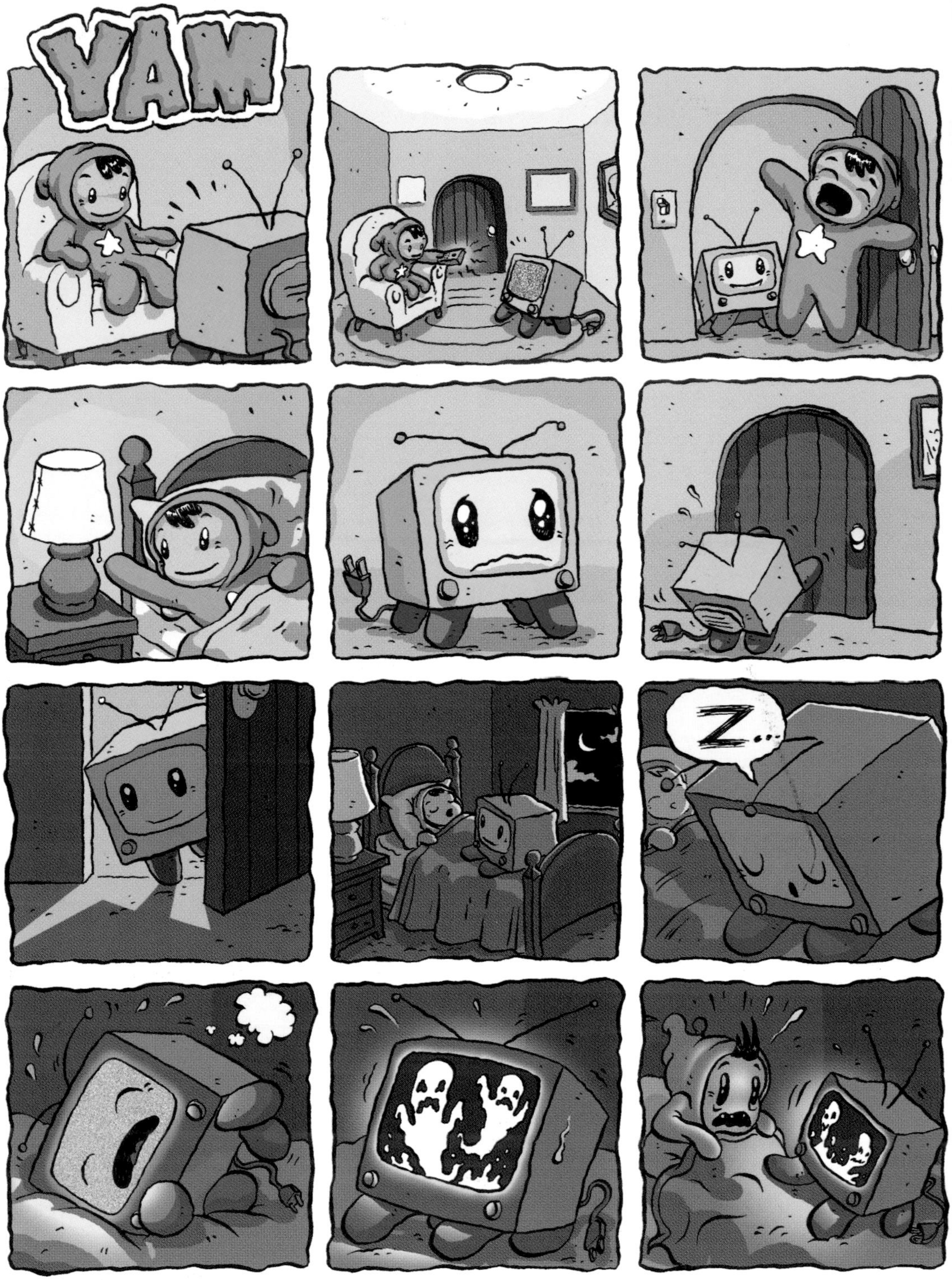
YAM
Z...

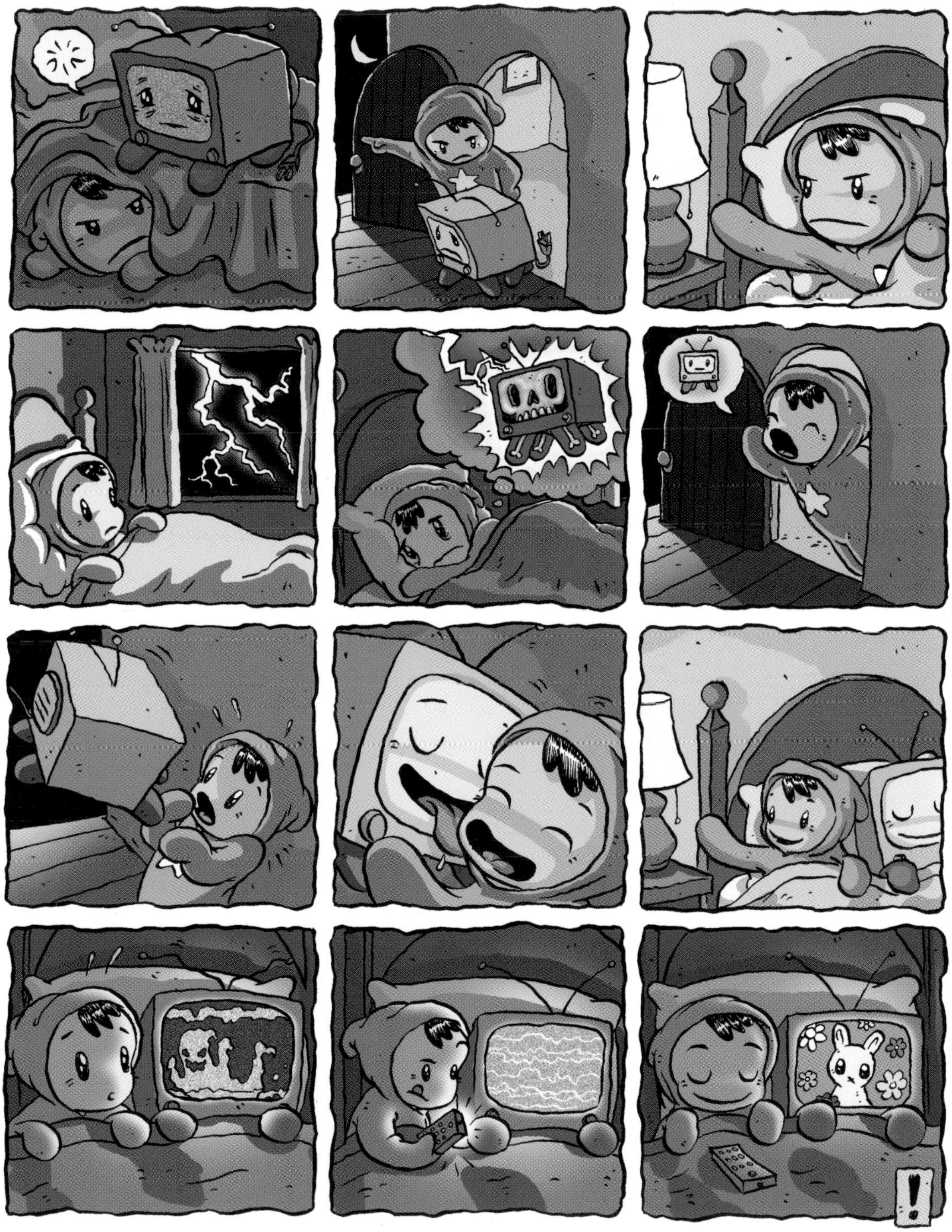
!

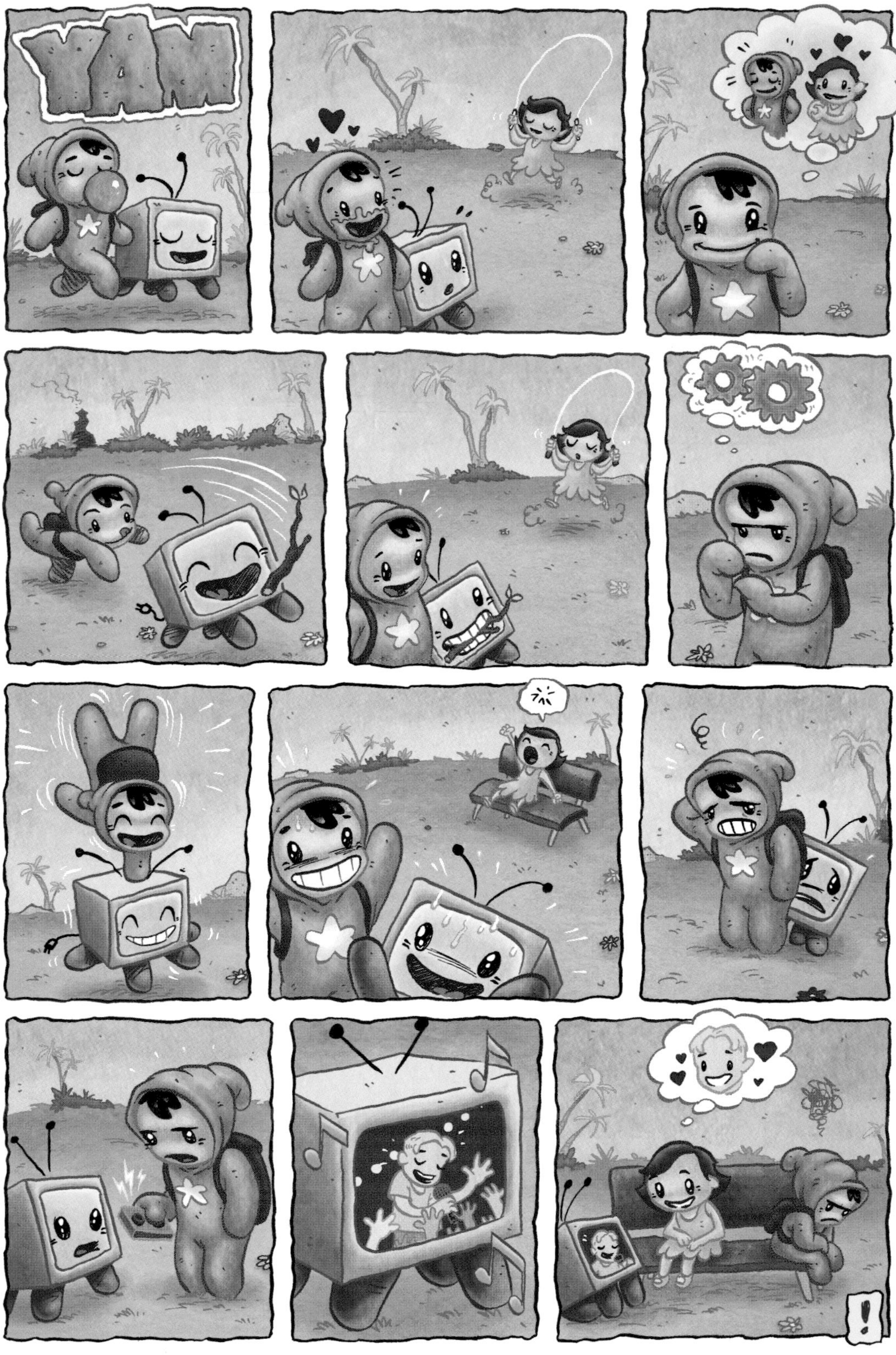
YAM
!

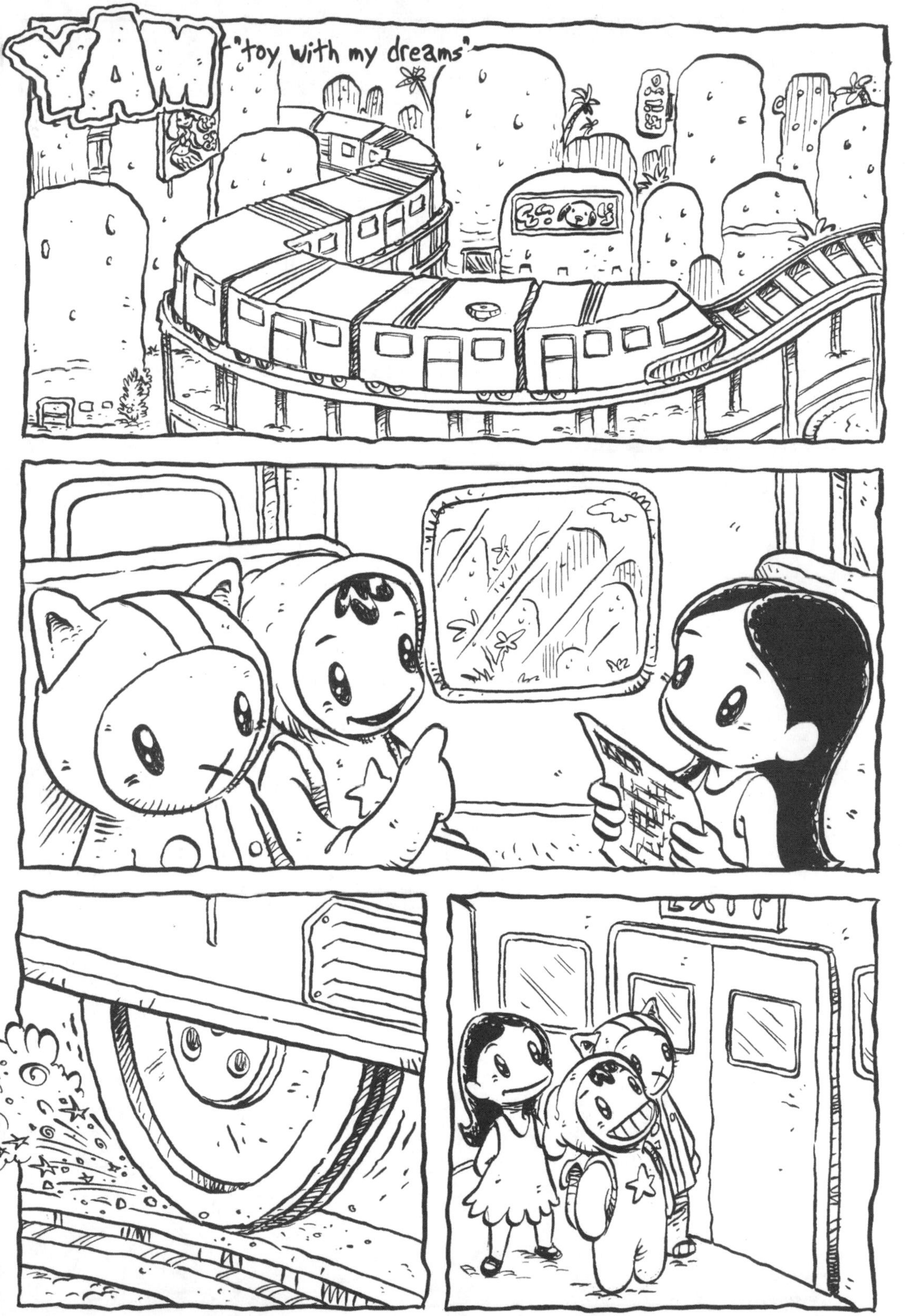
YAM
"toy with my dreams"

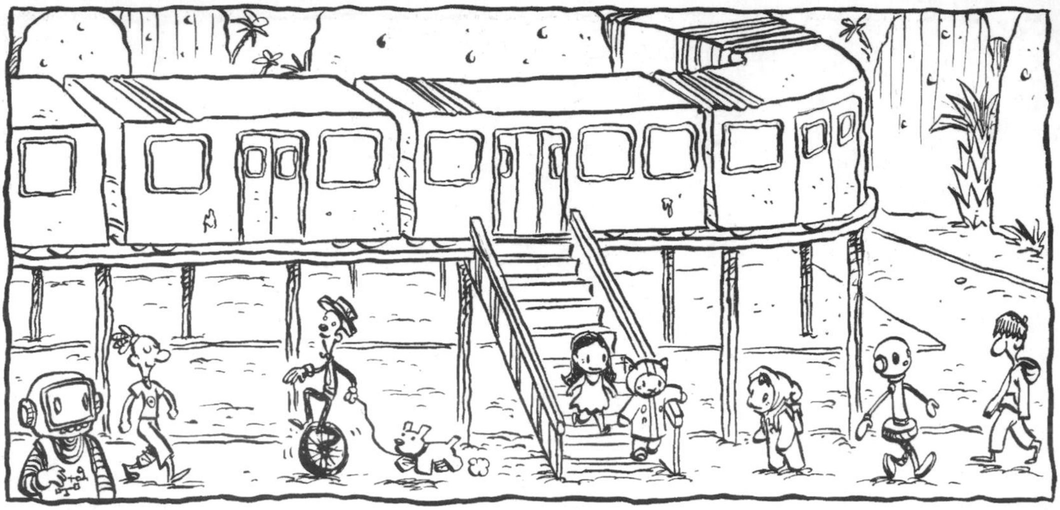

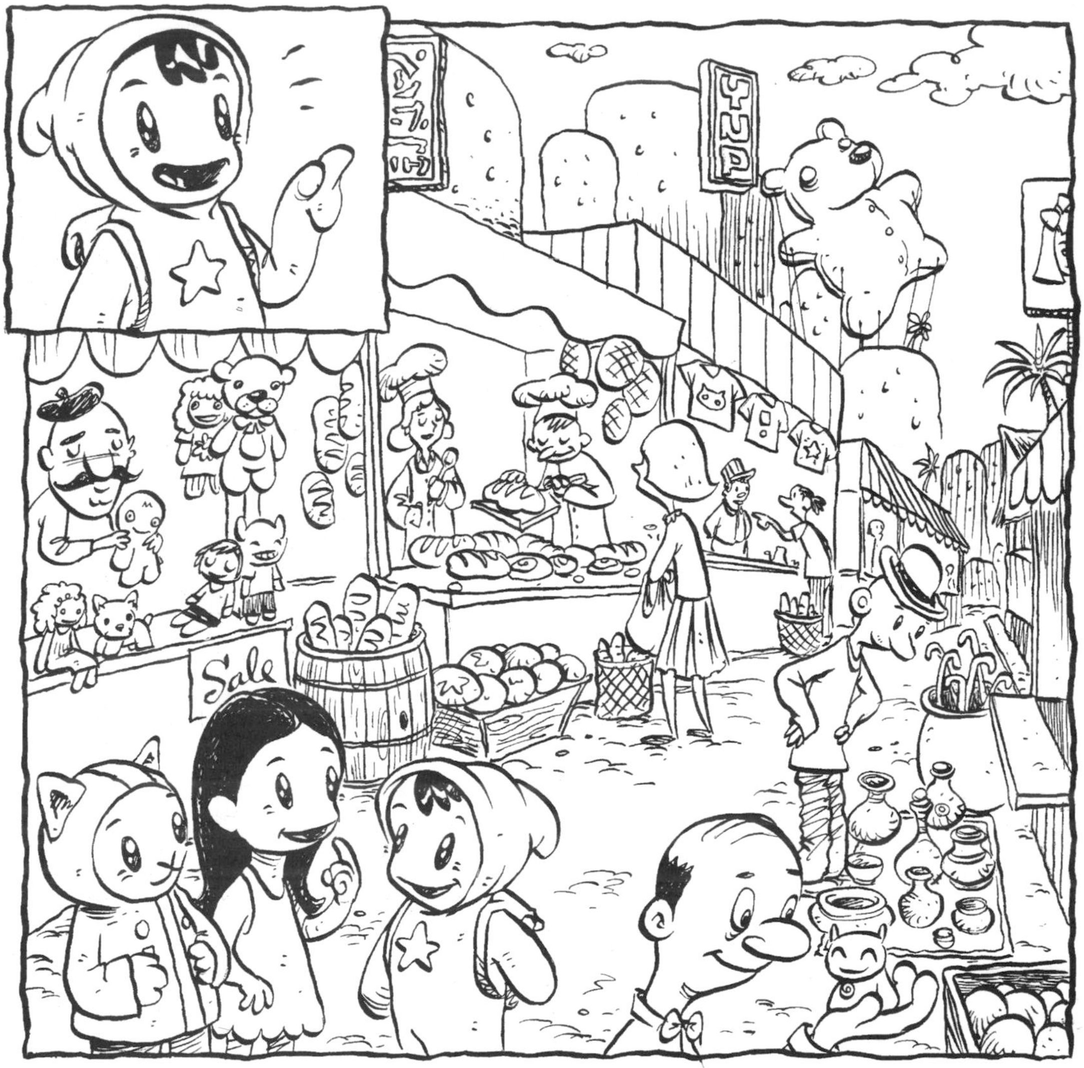
Sale

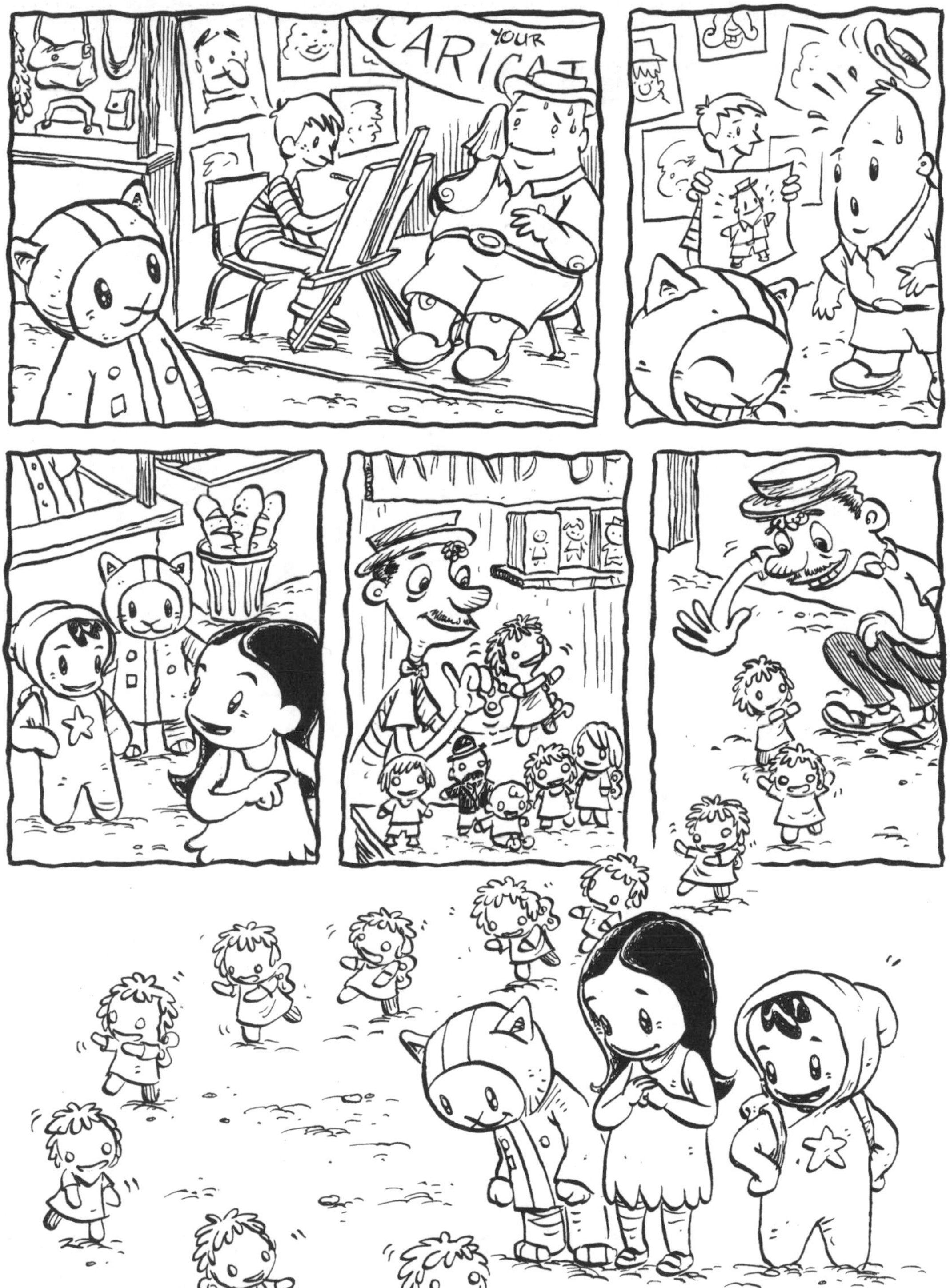
YOUR
CARICAT

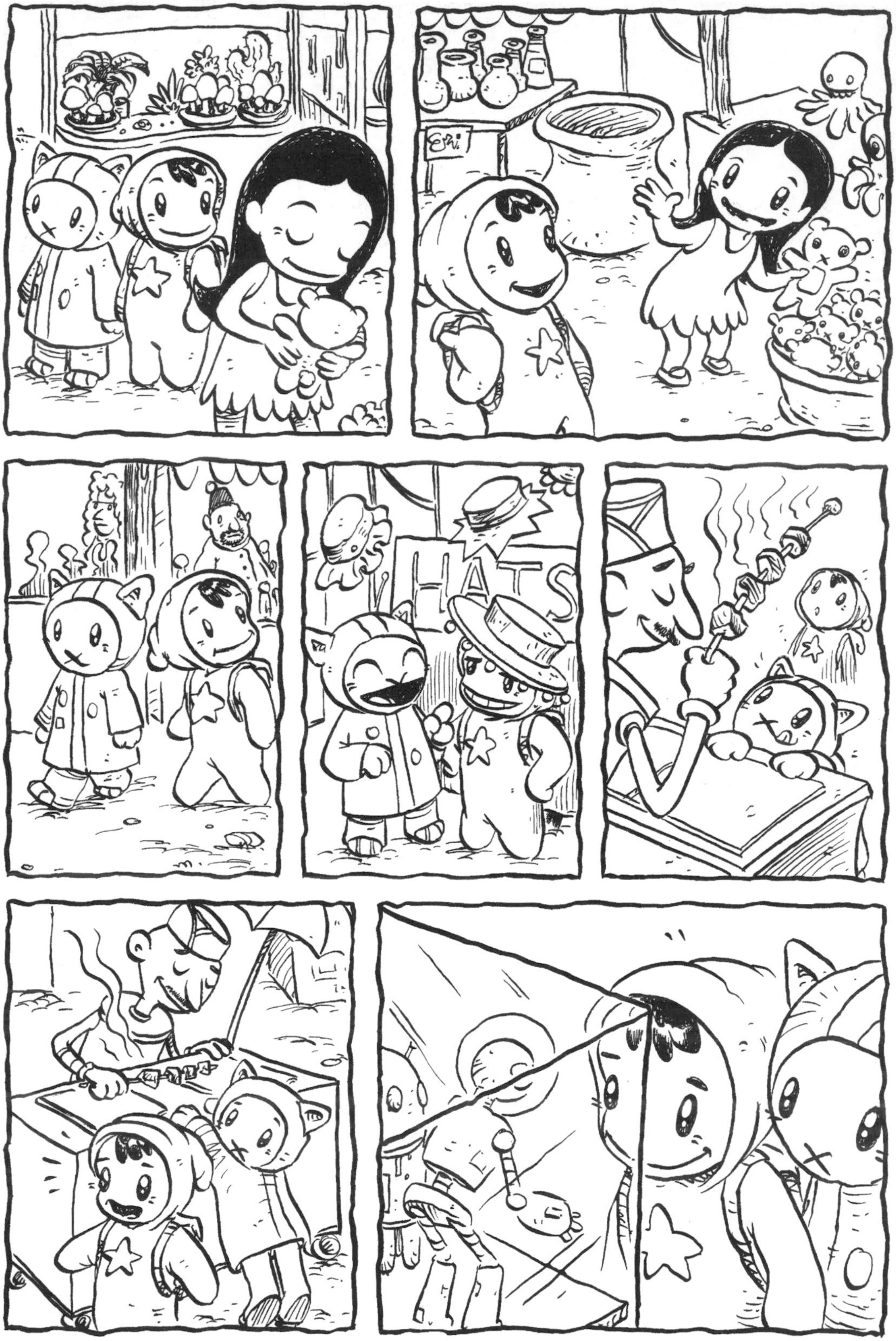
HATS

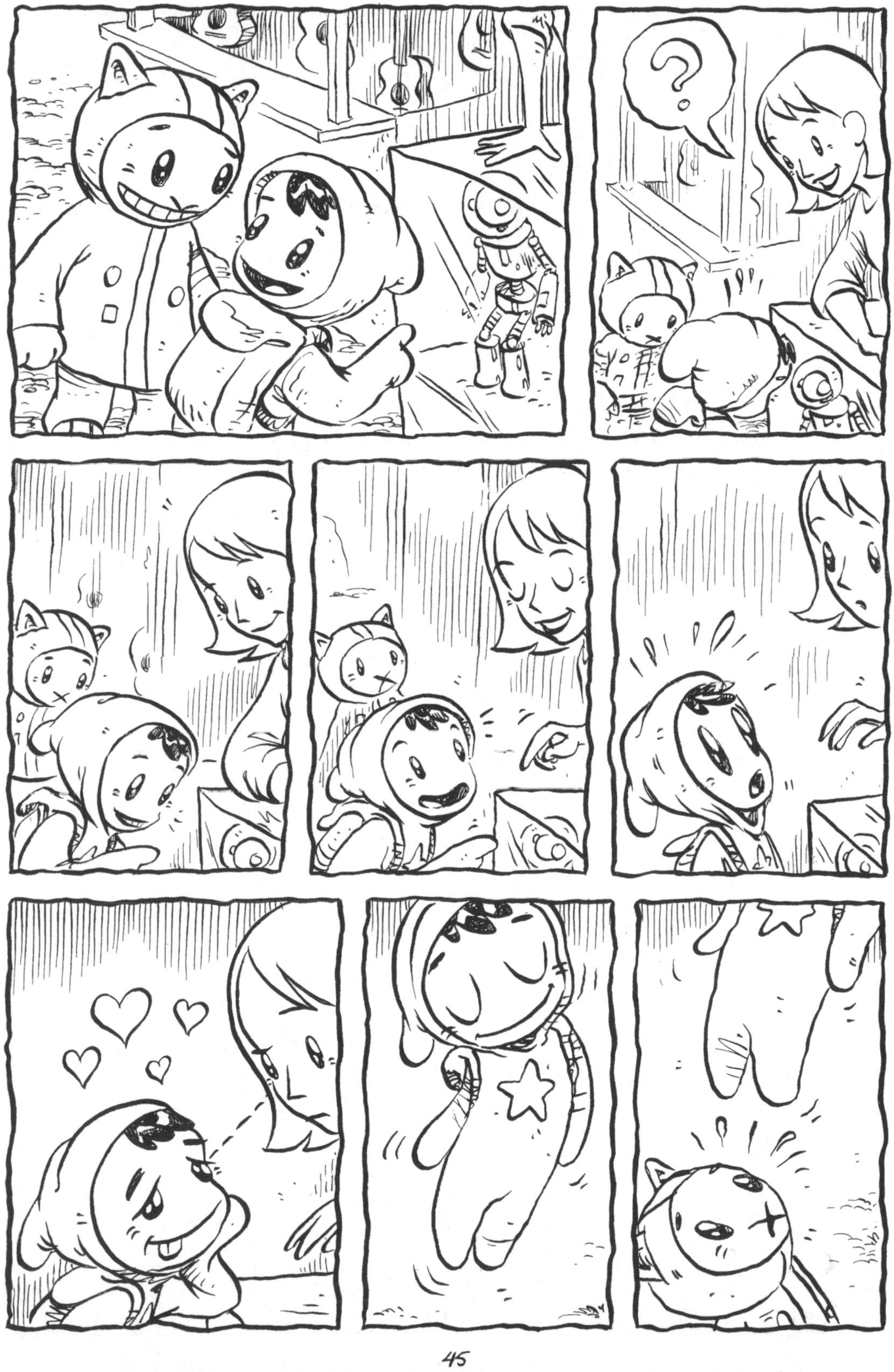
?

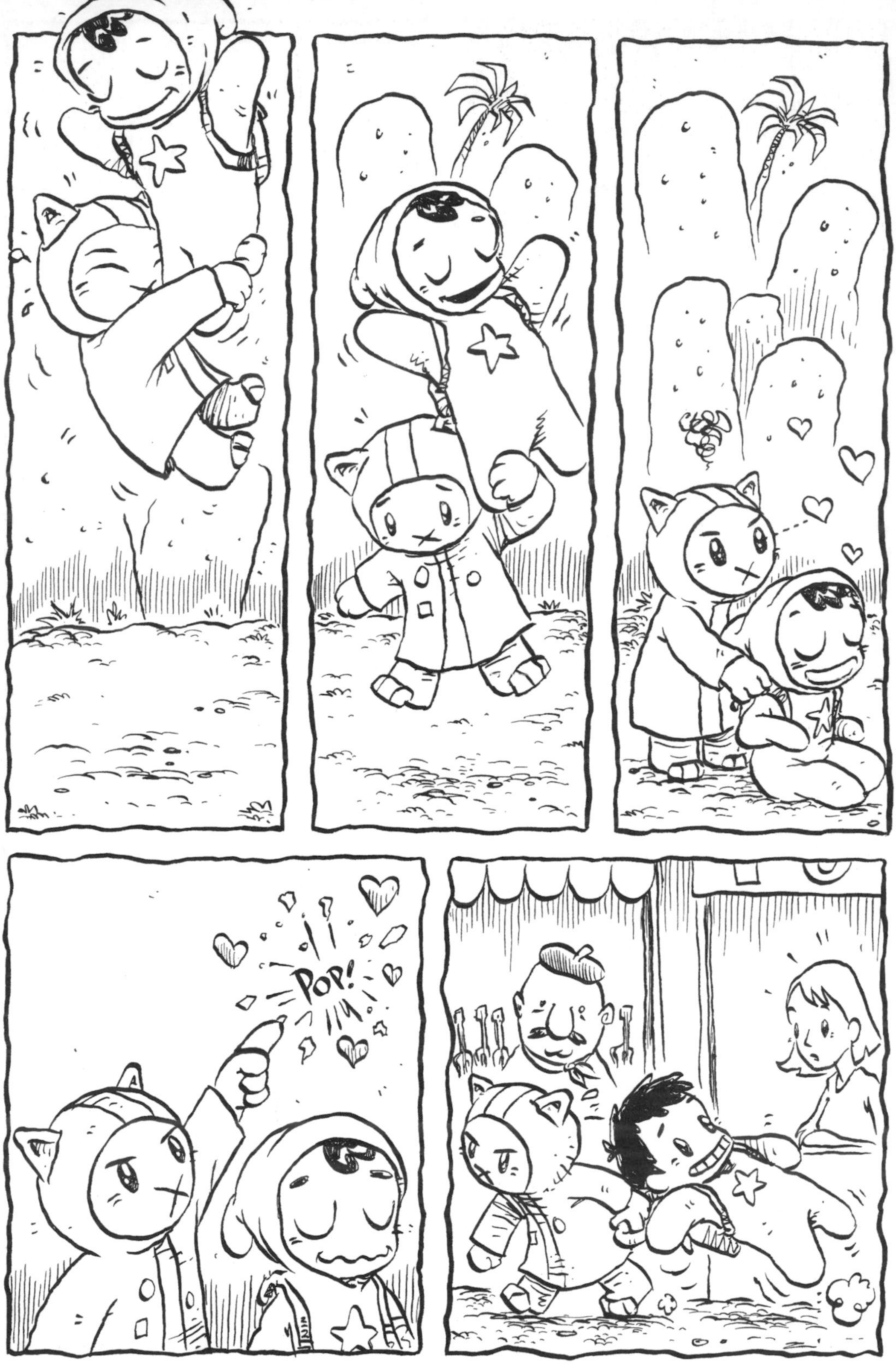
POP!

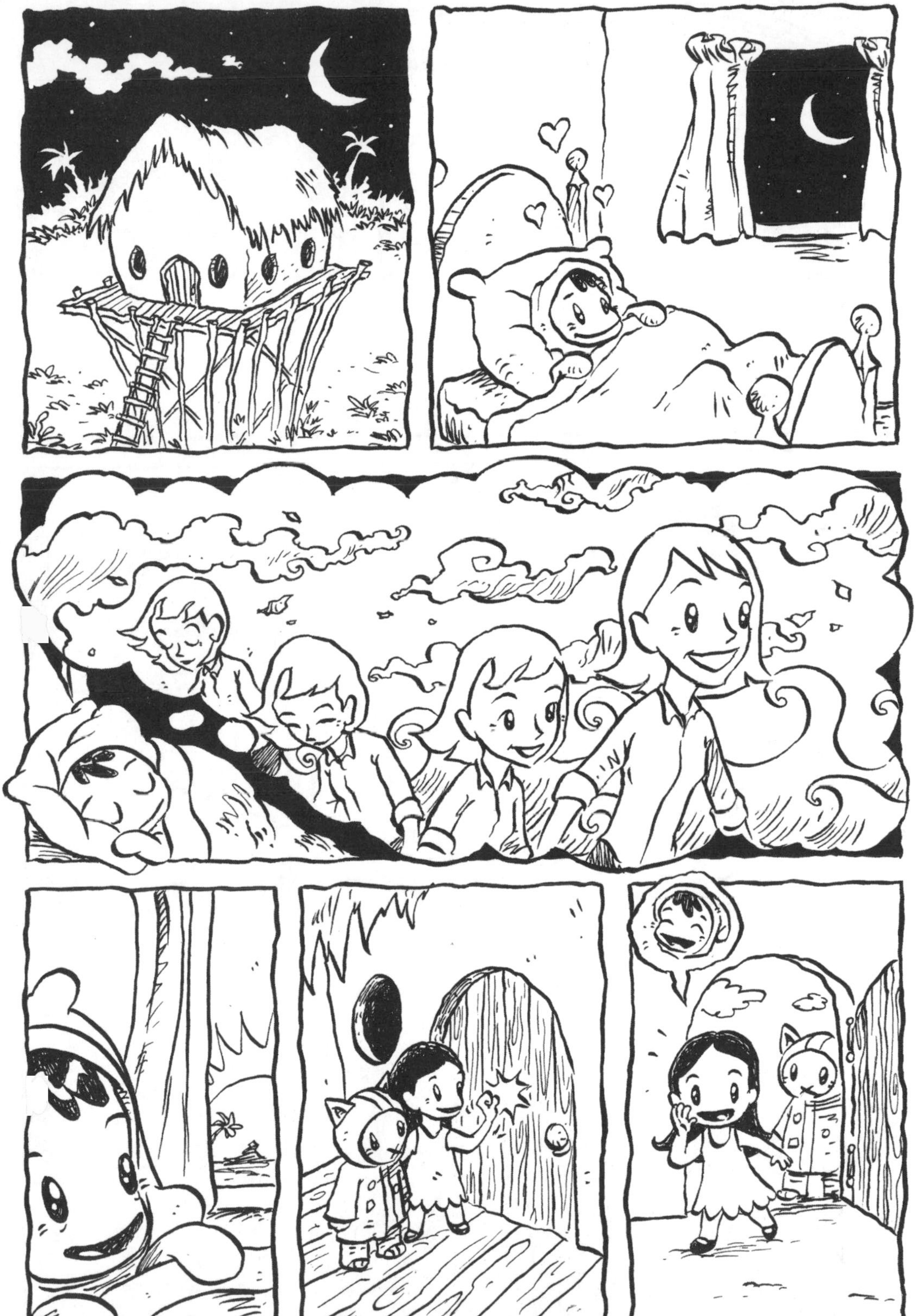

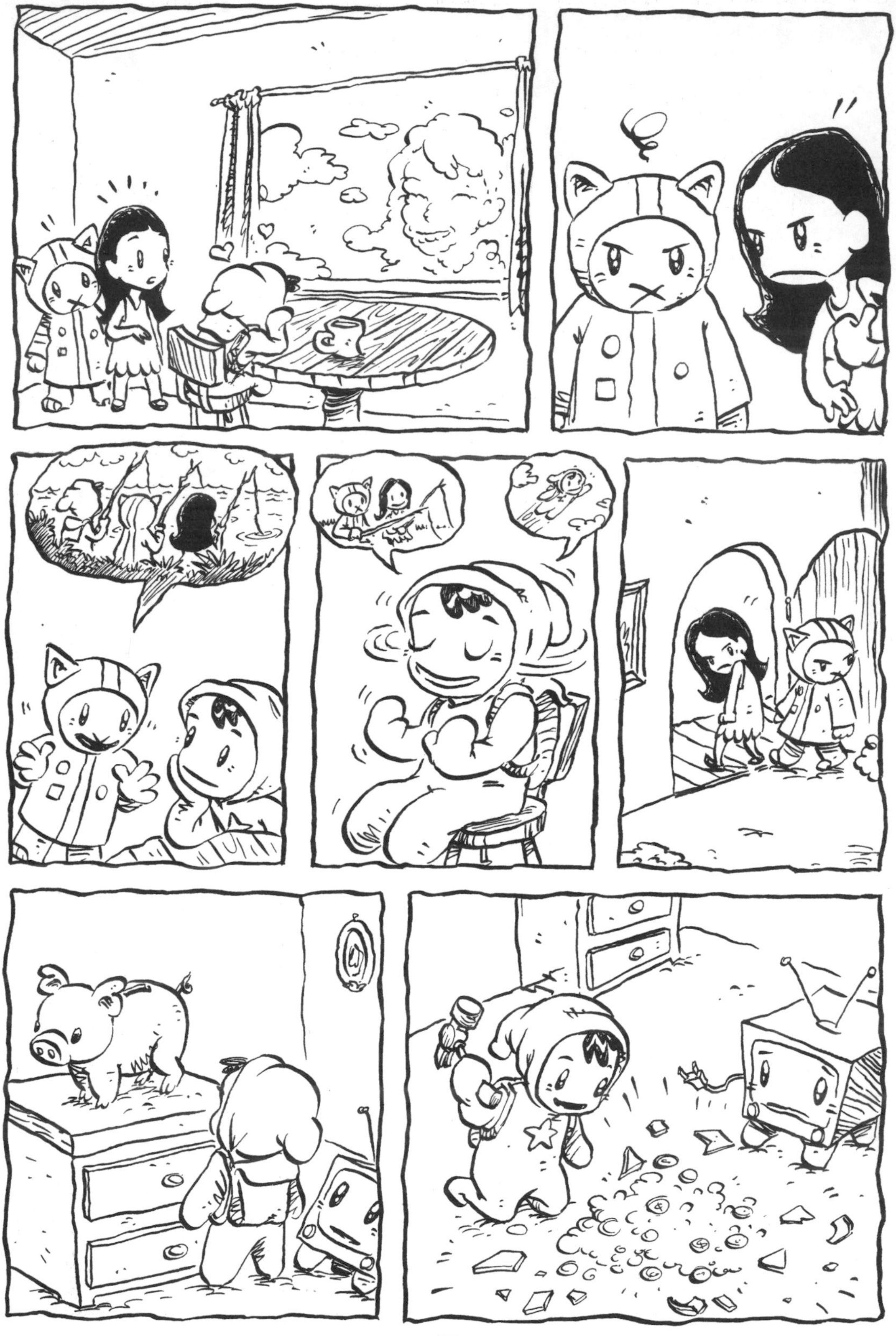

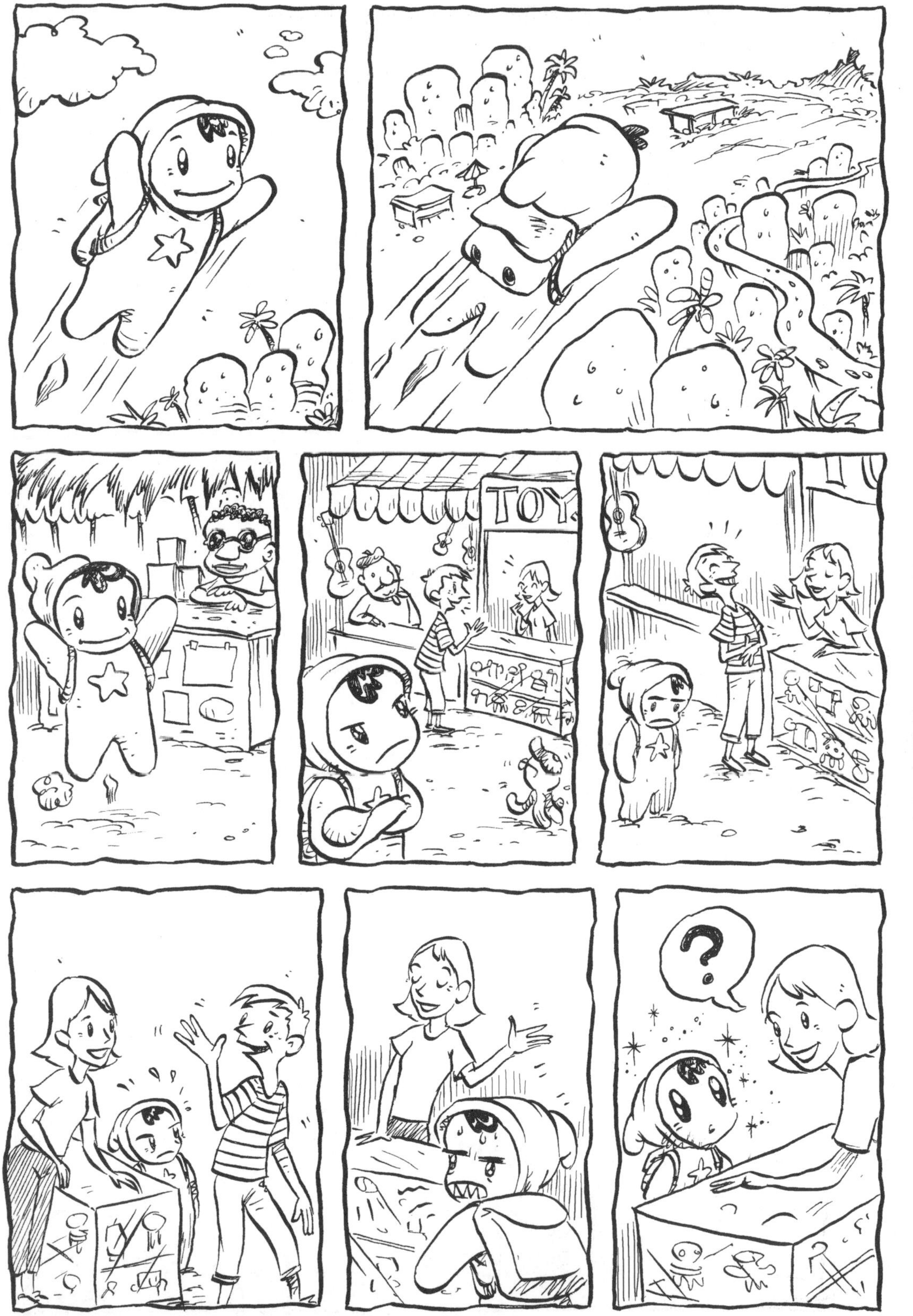
TOY
?

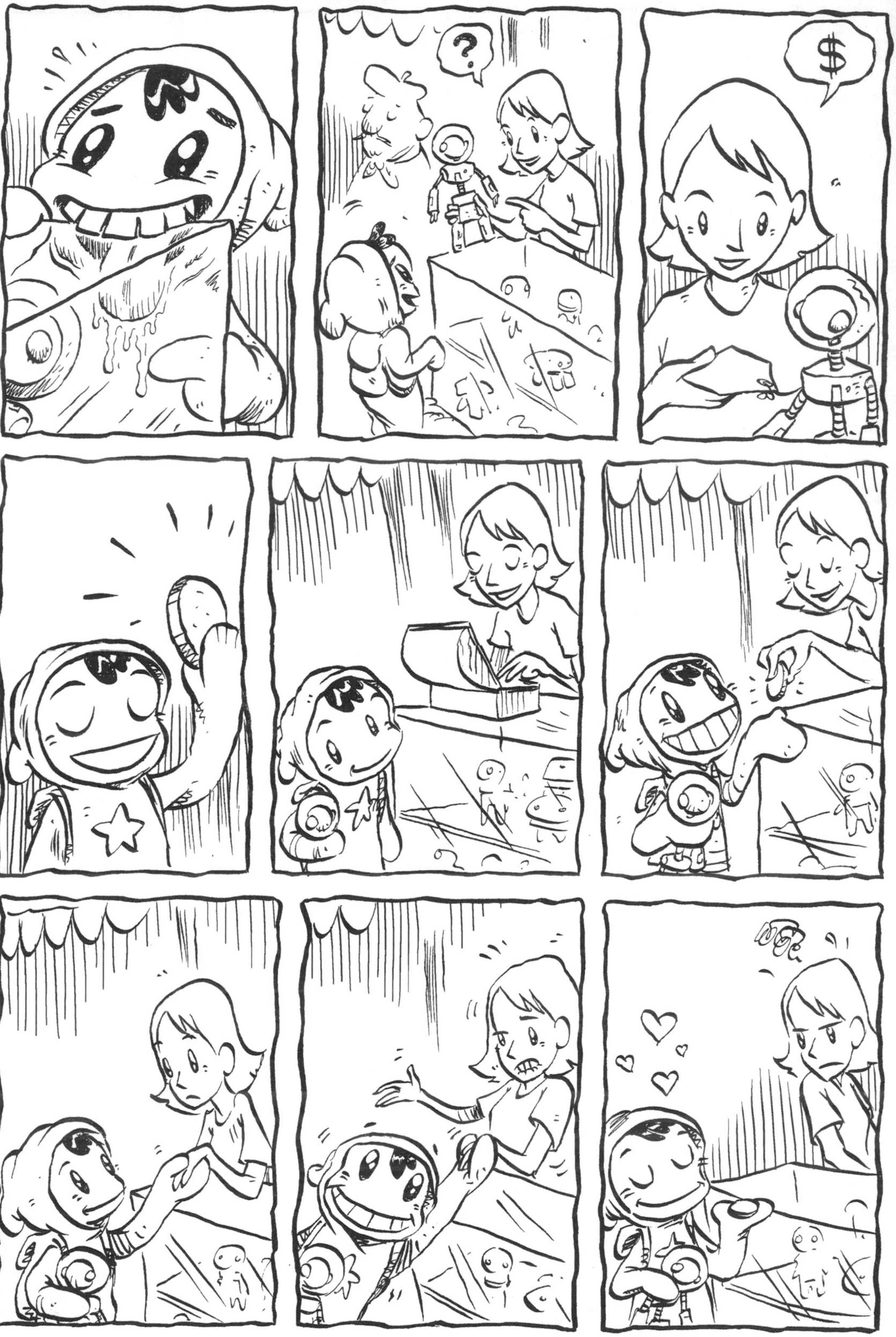
?
$

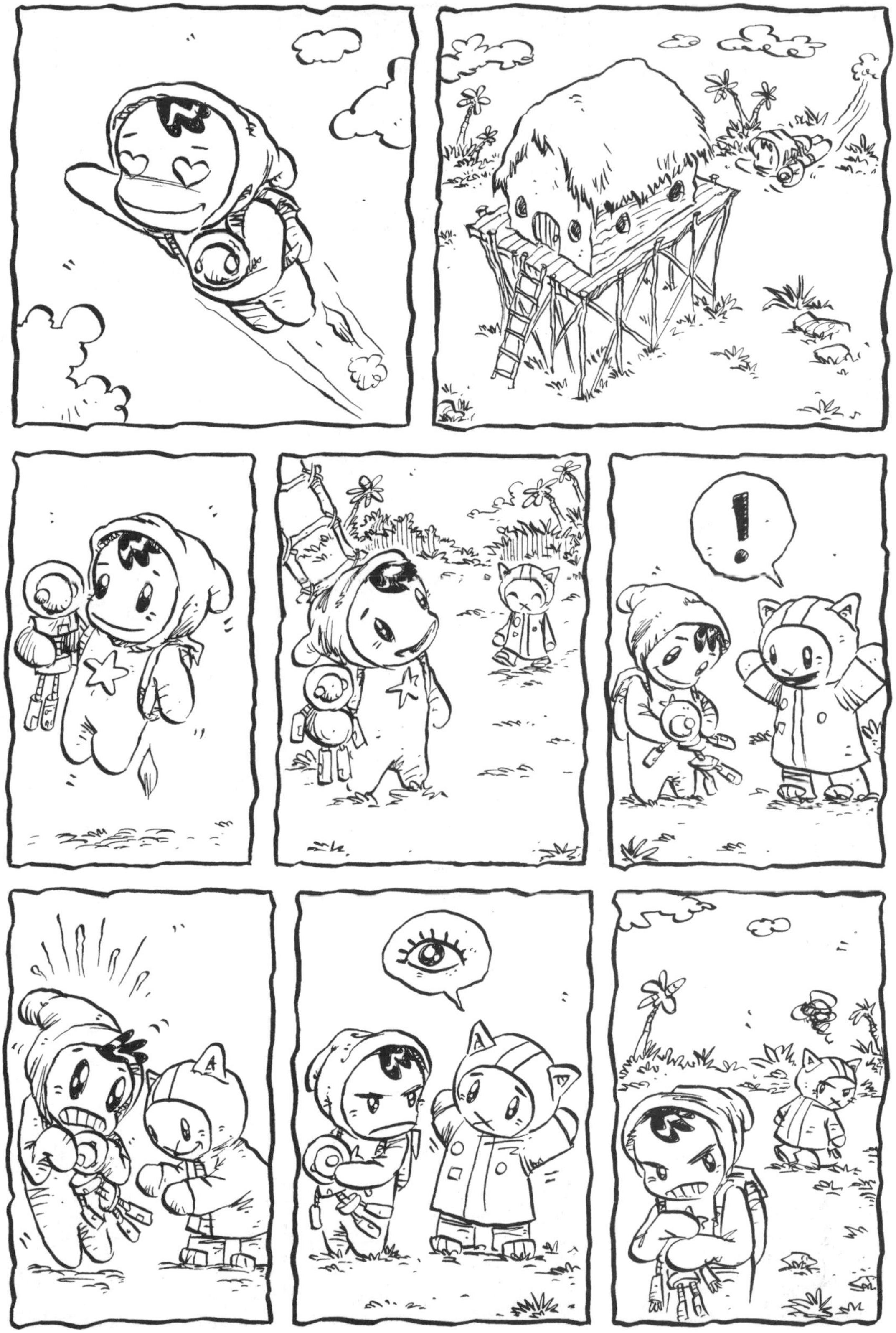

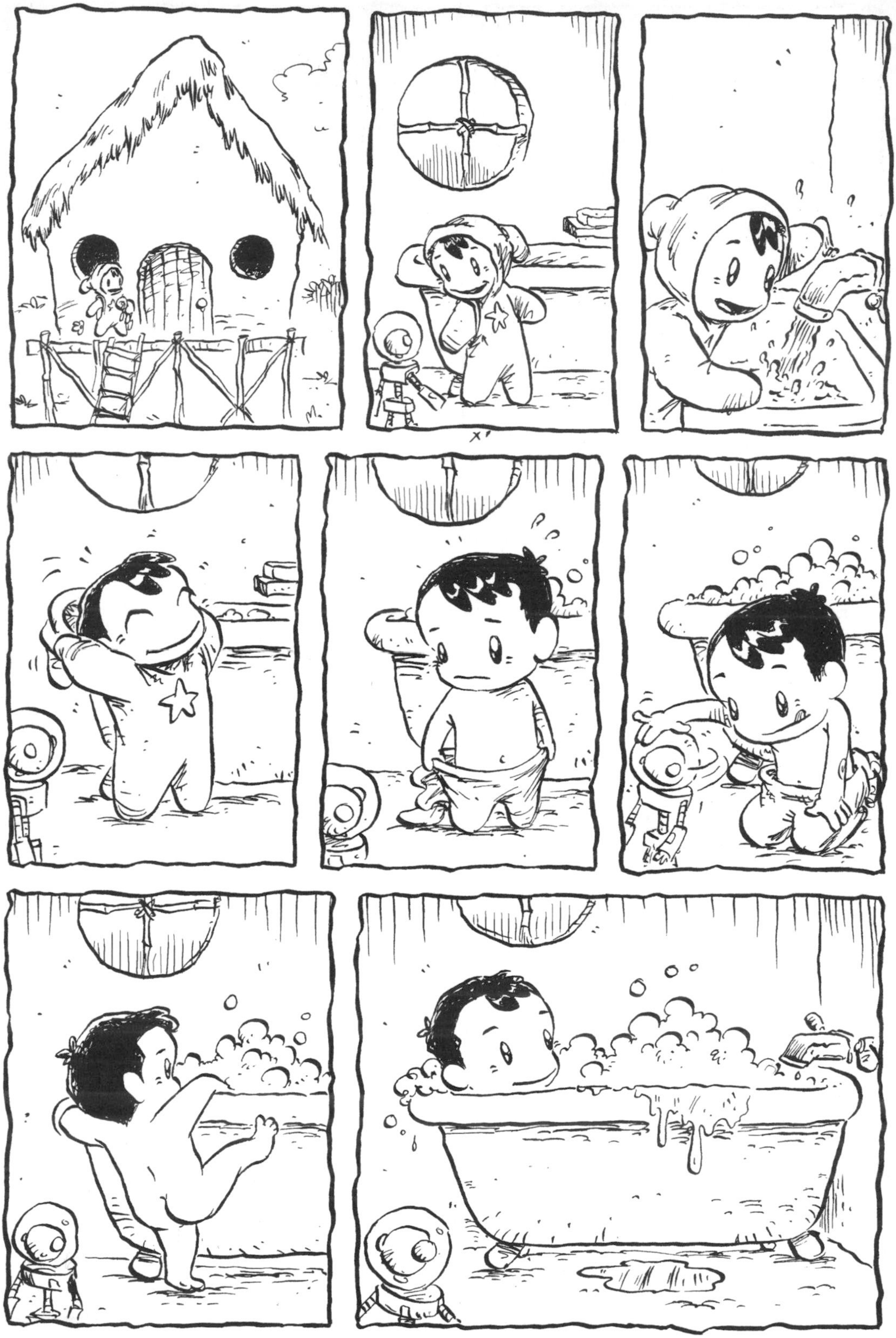

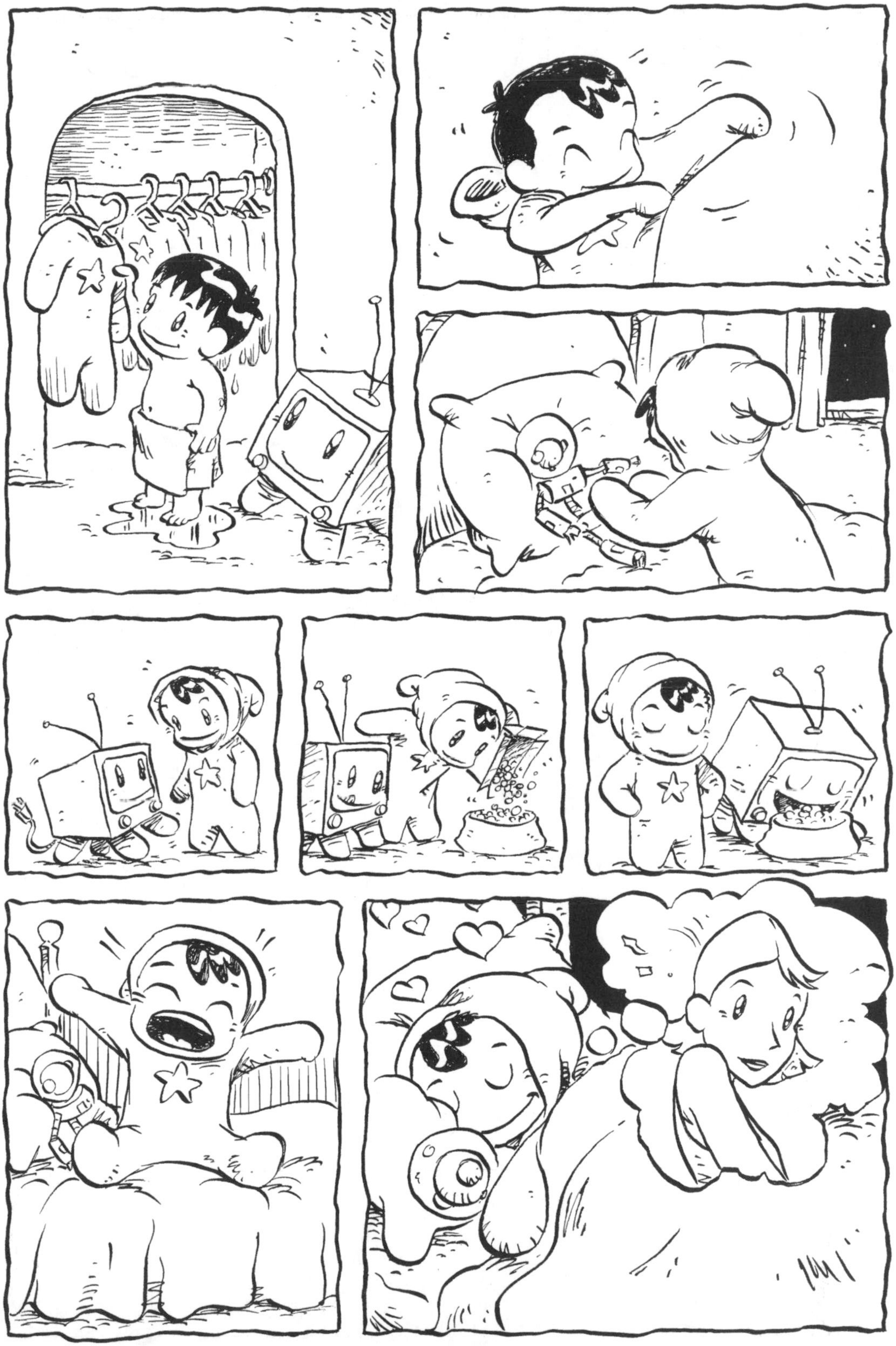

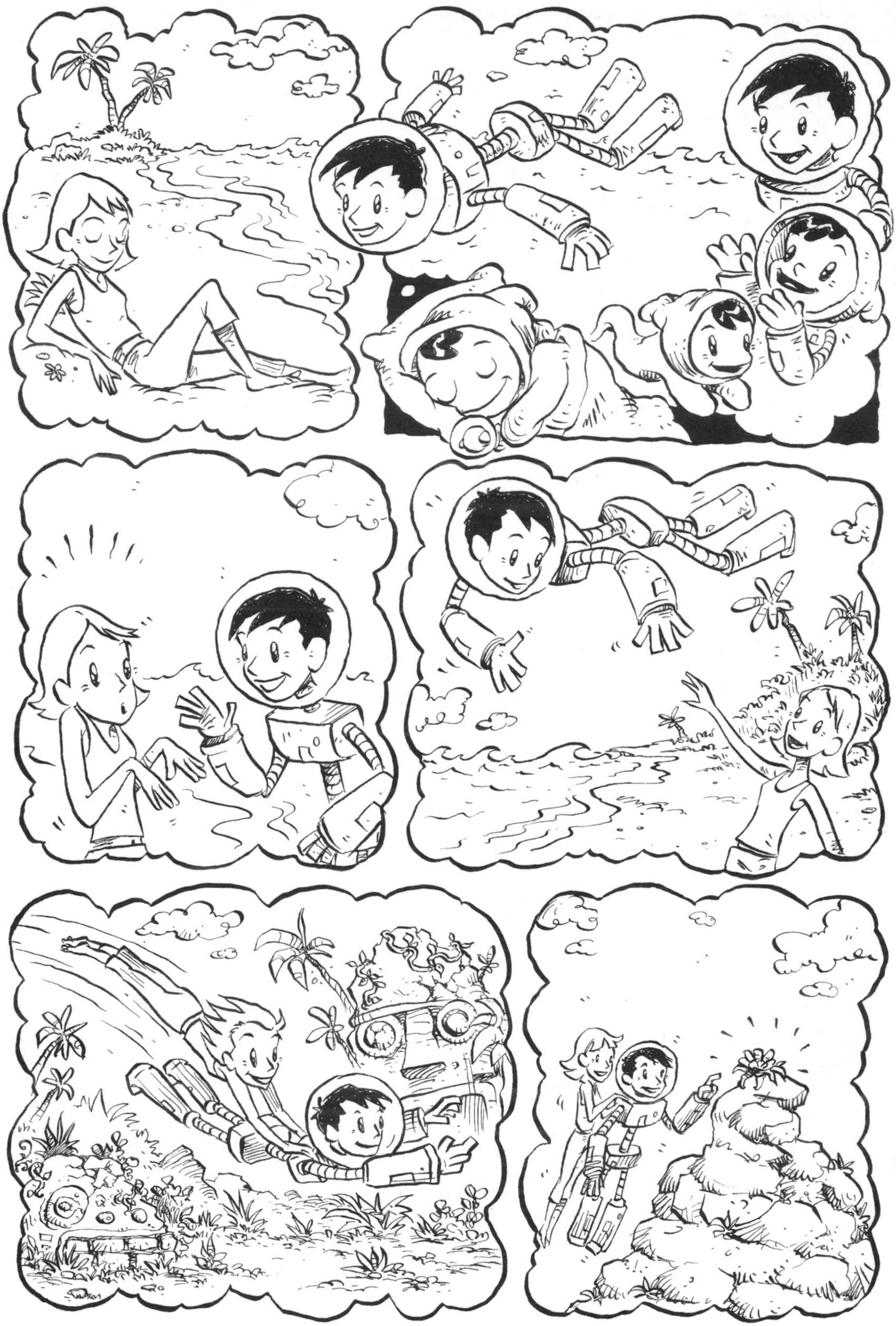

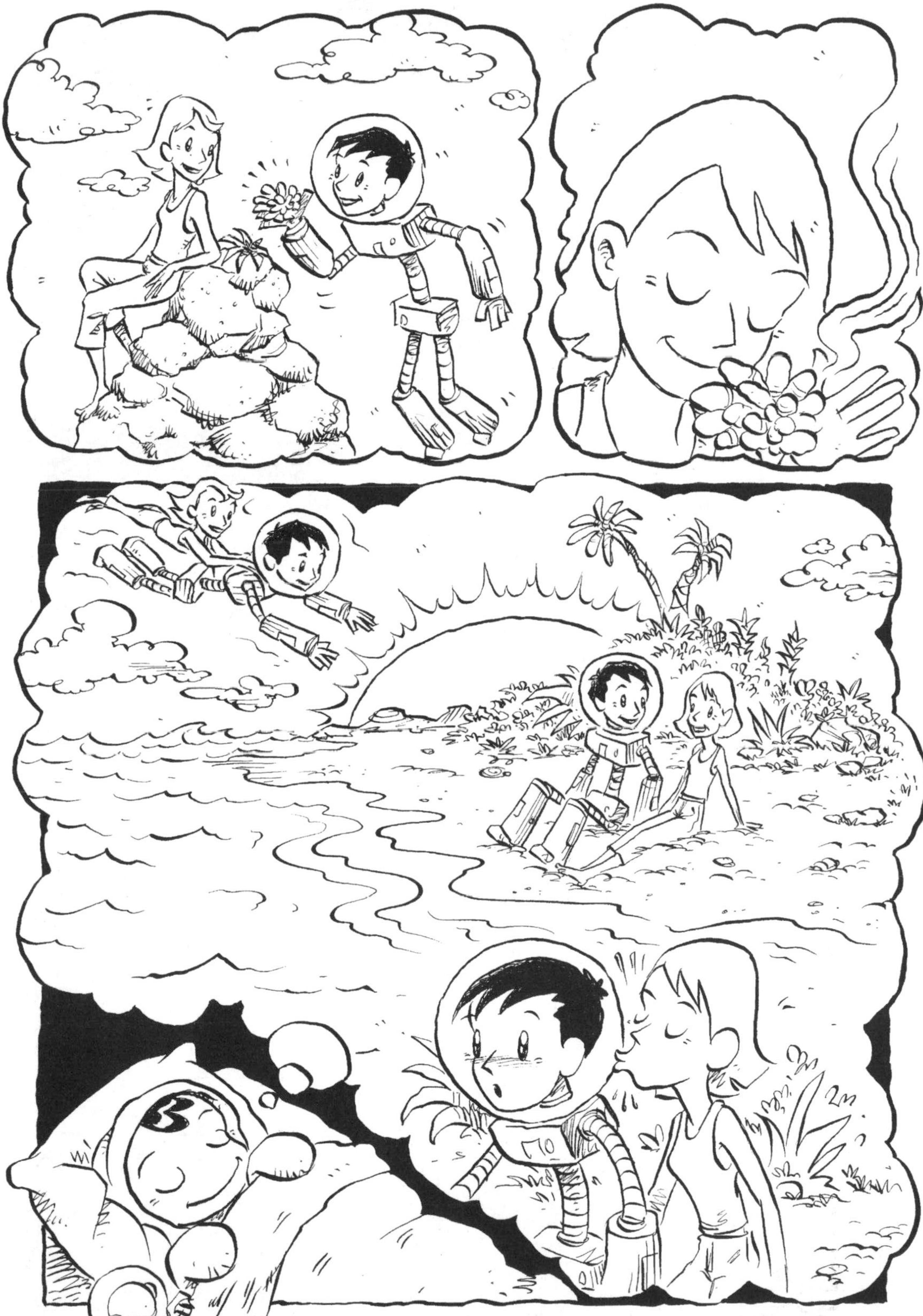

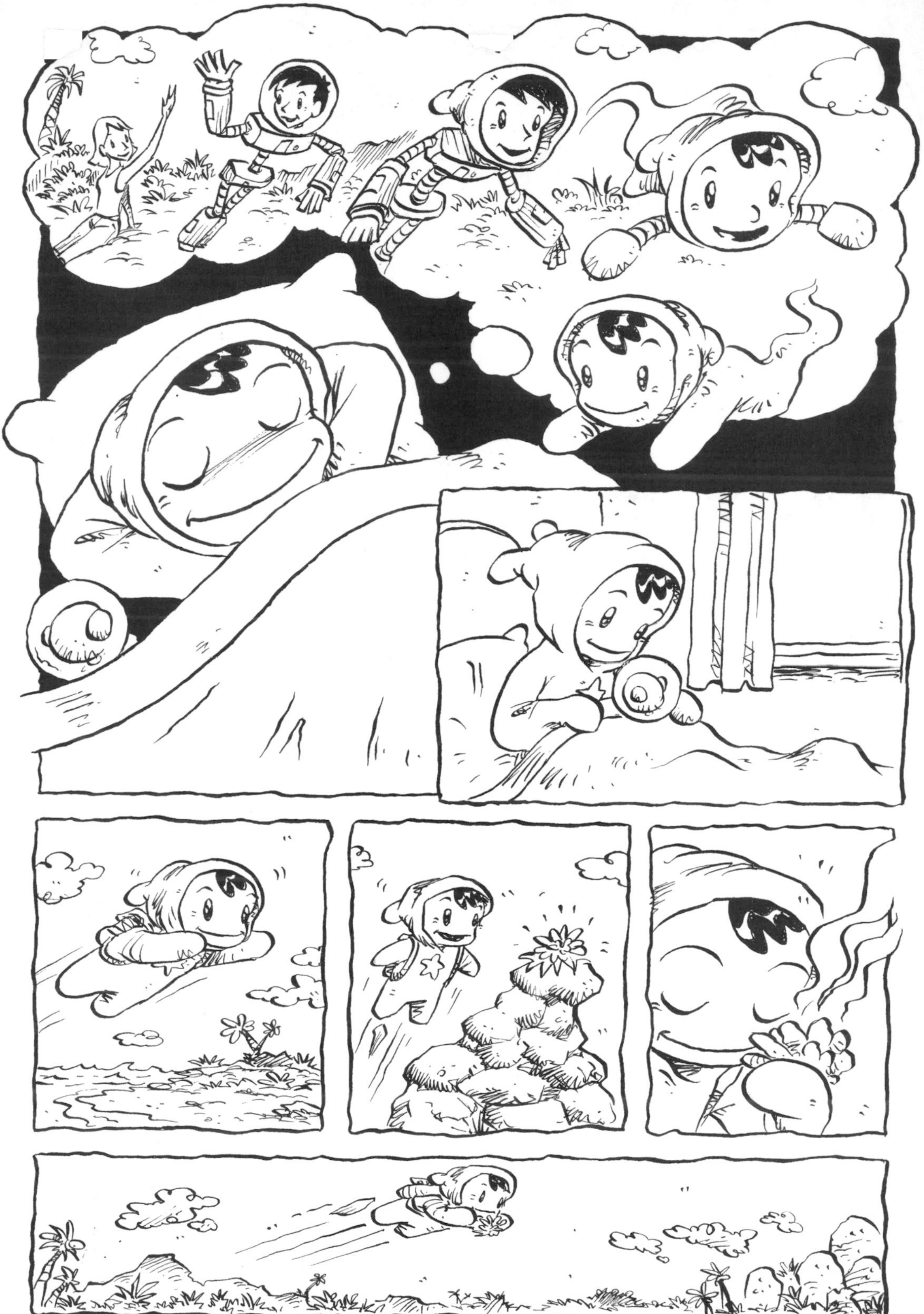

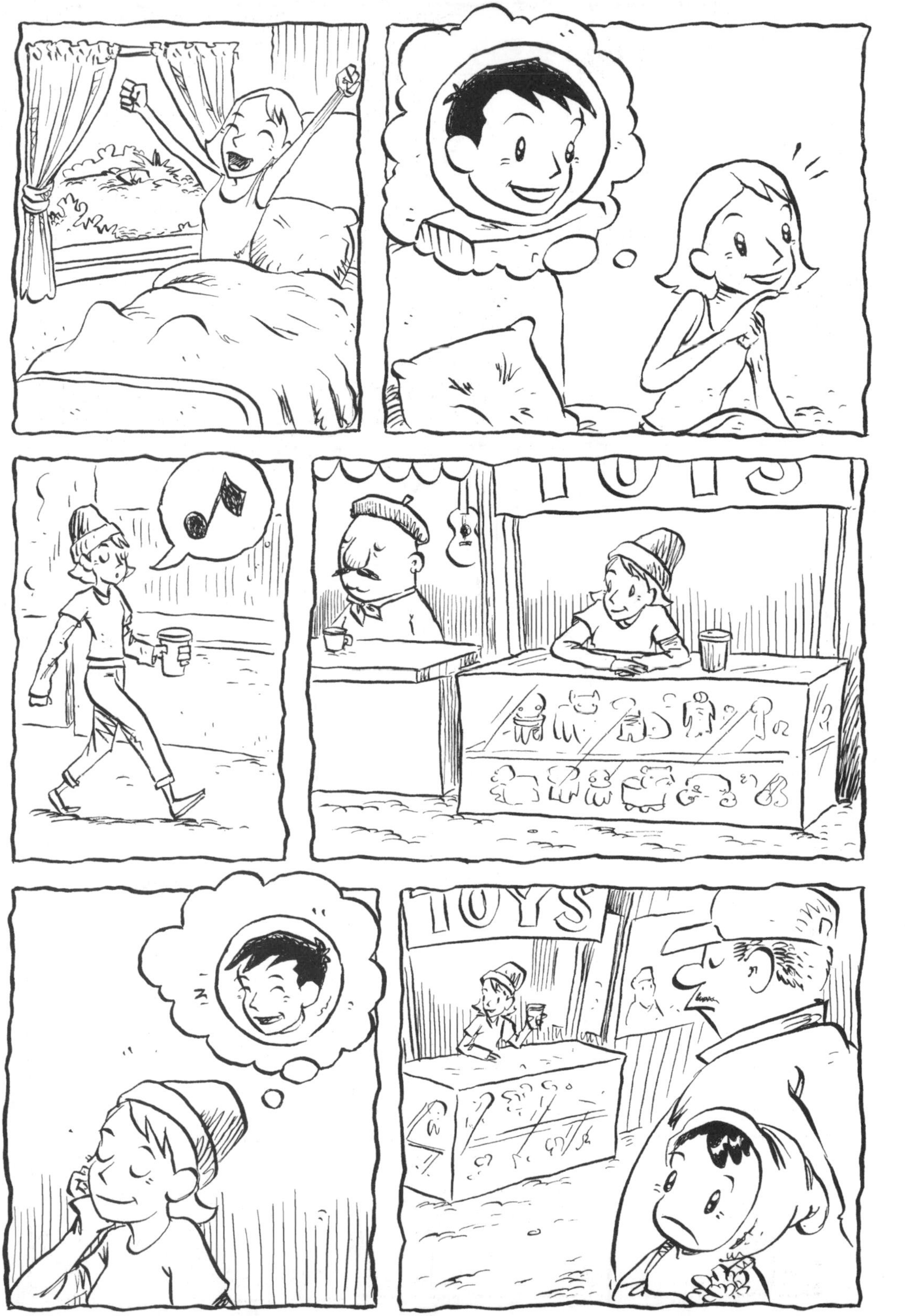
TOYS
TOYS

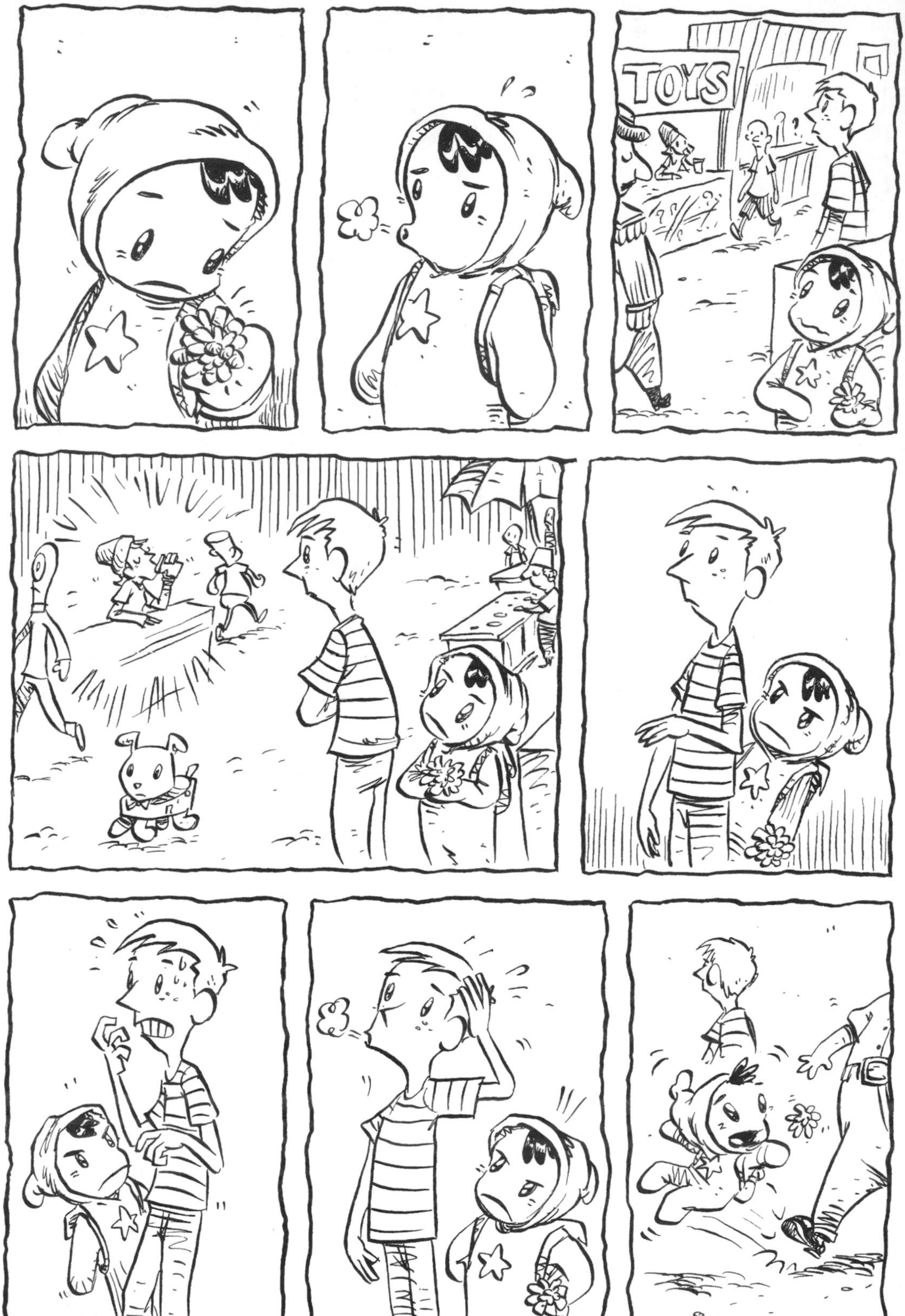
TOYS

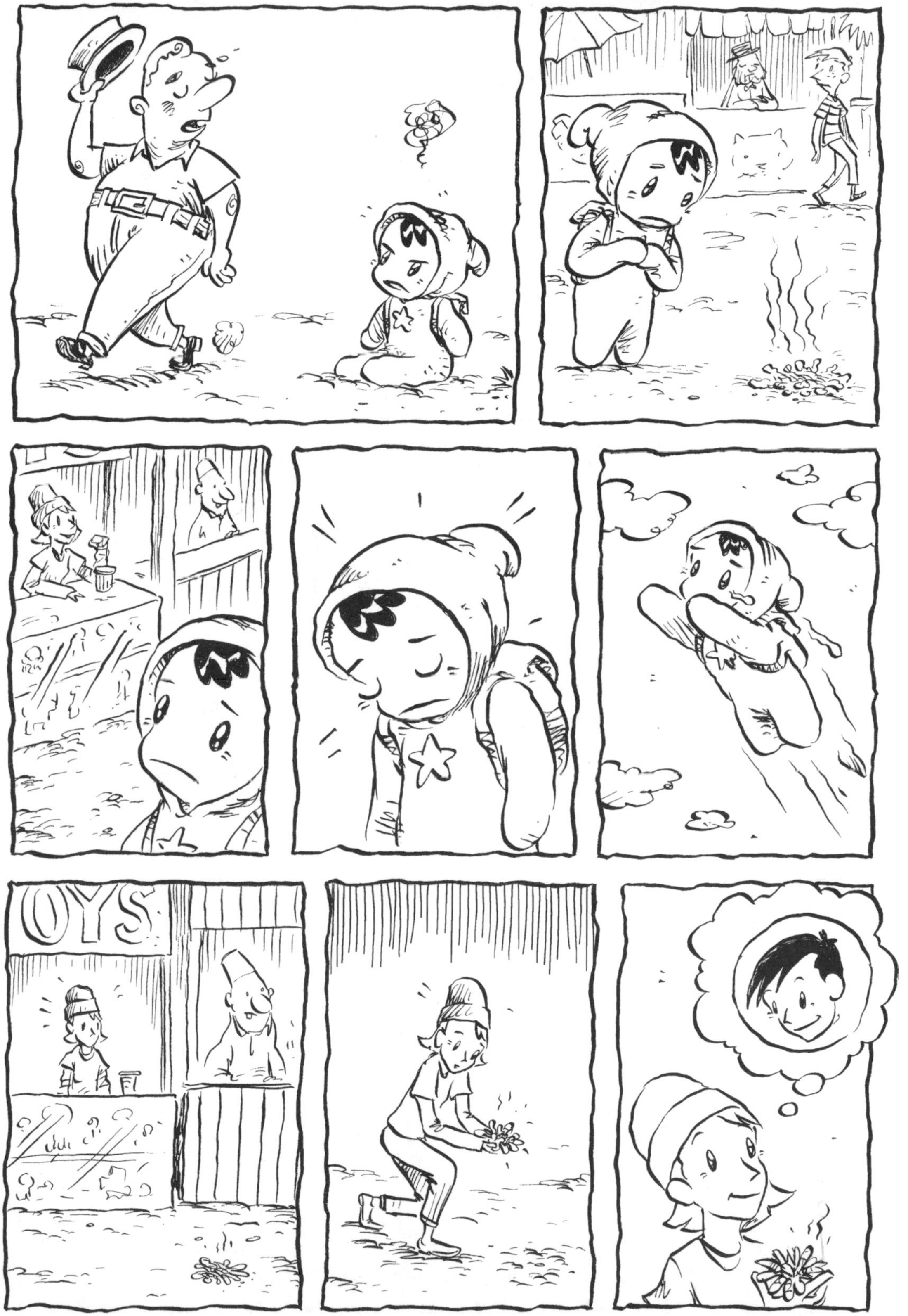
OYS

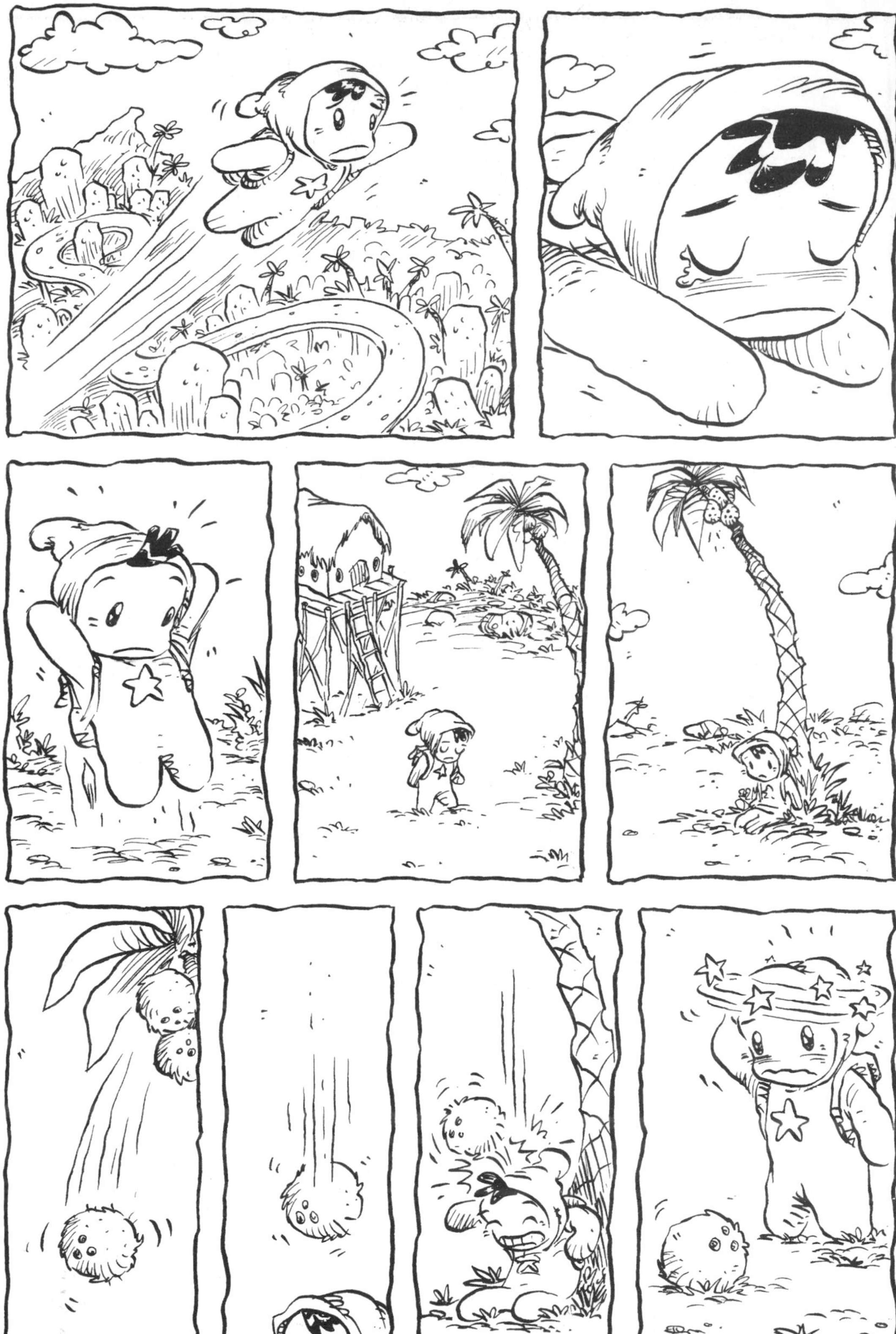

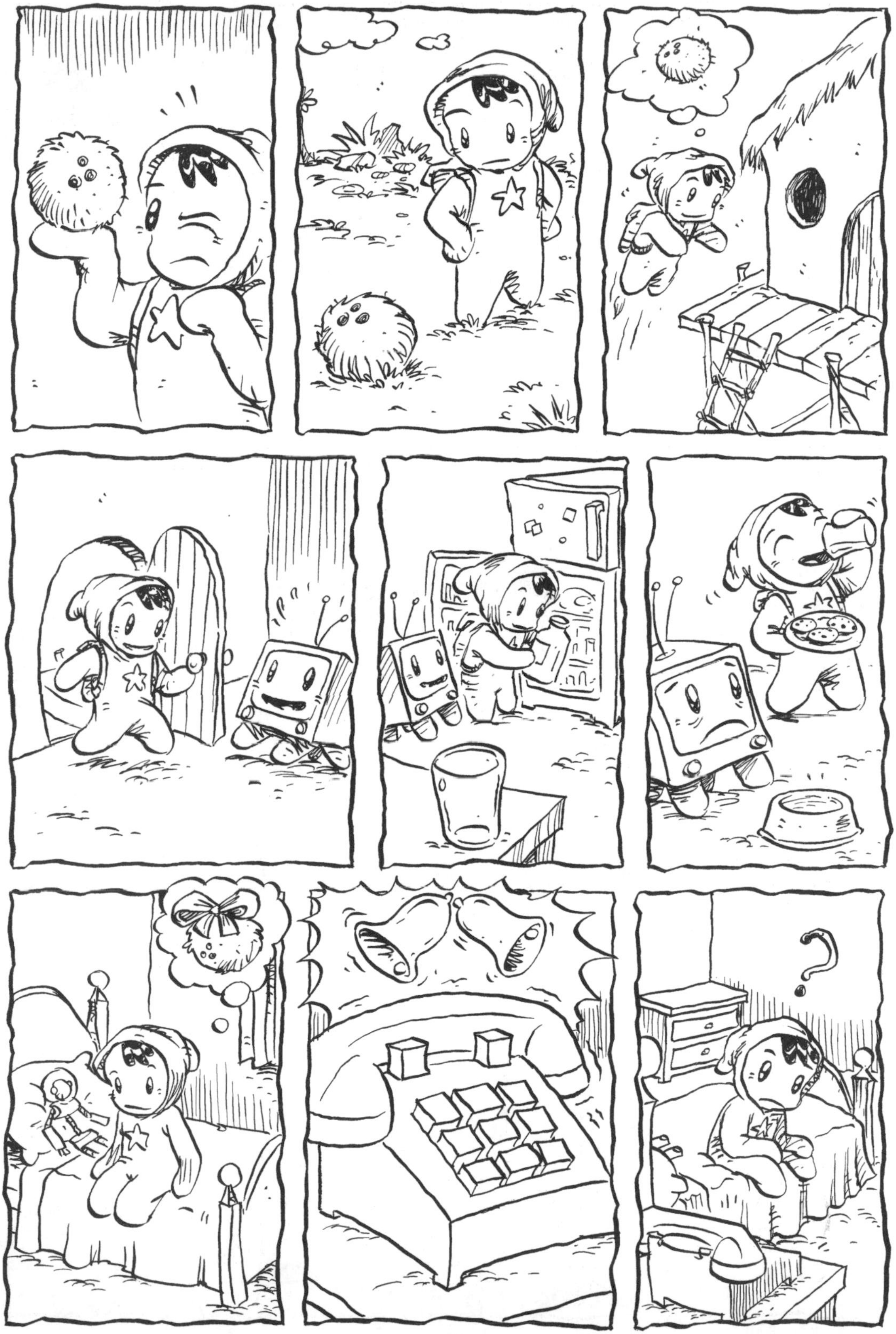

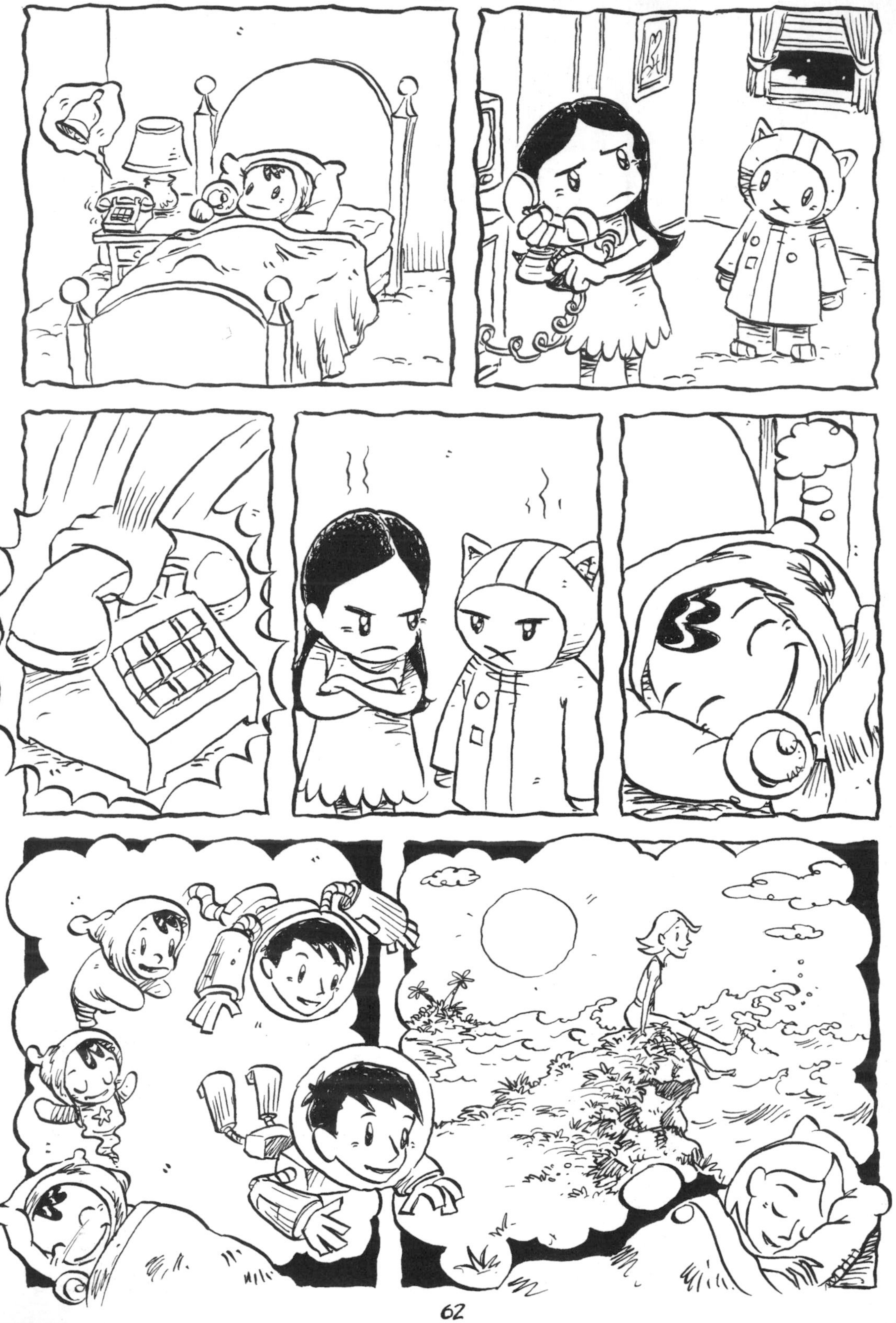

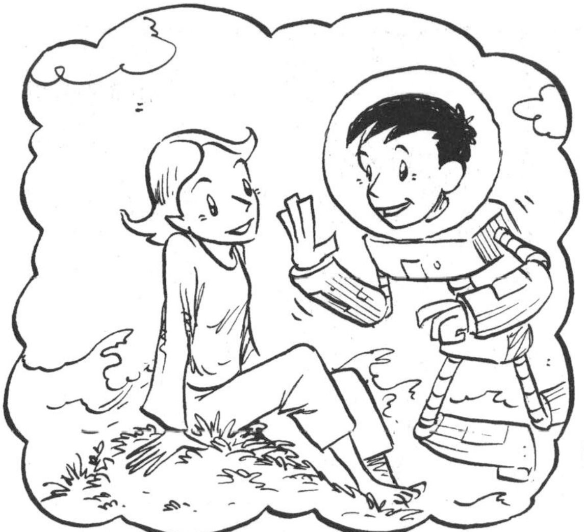

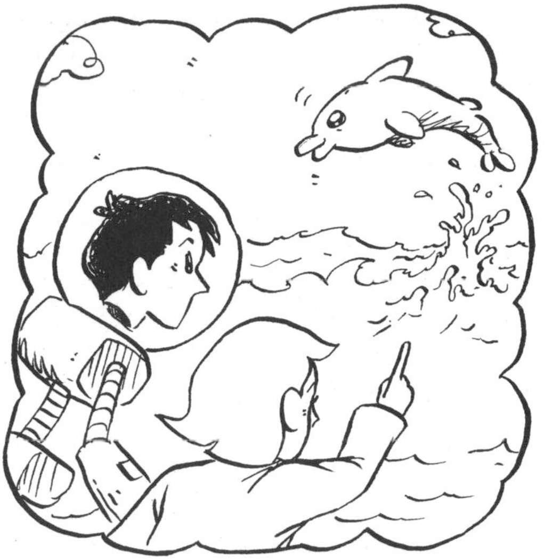

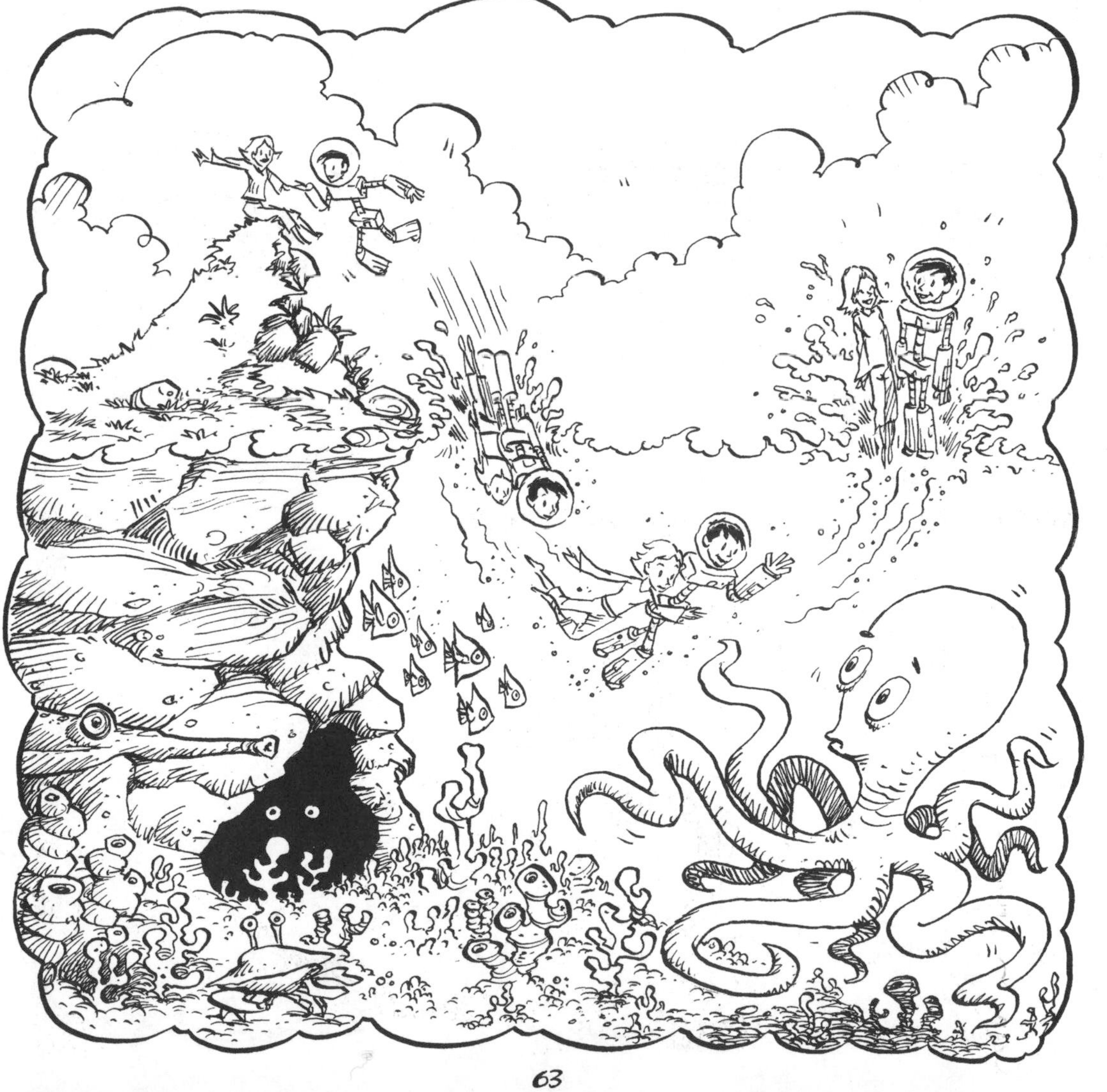

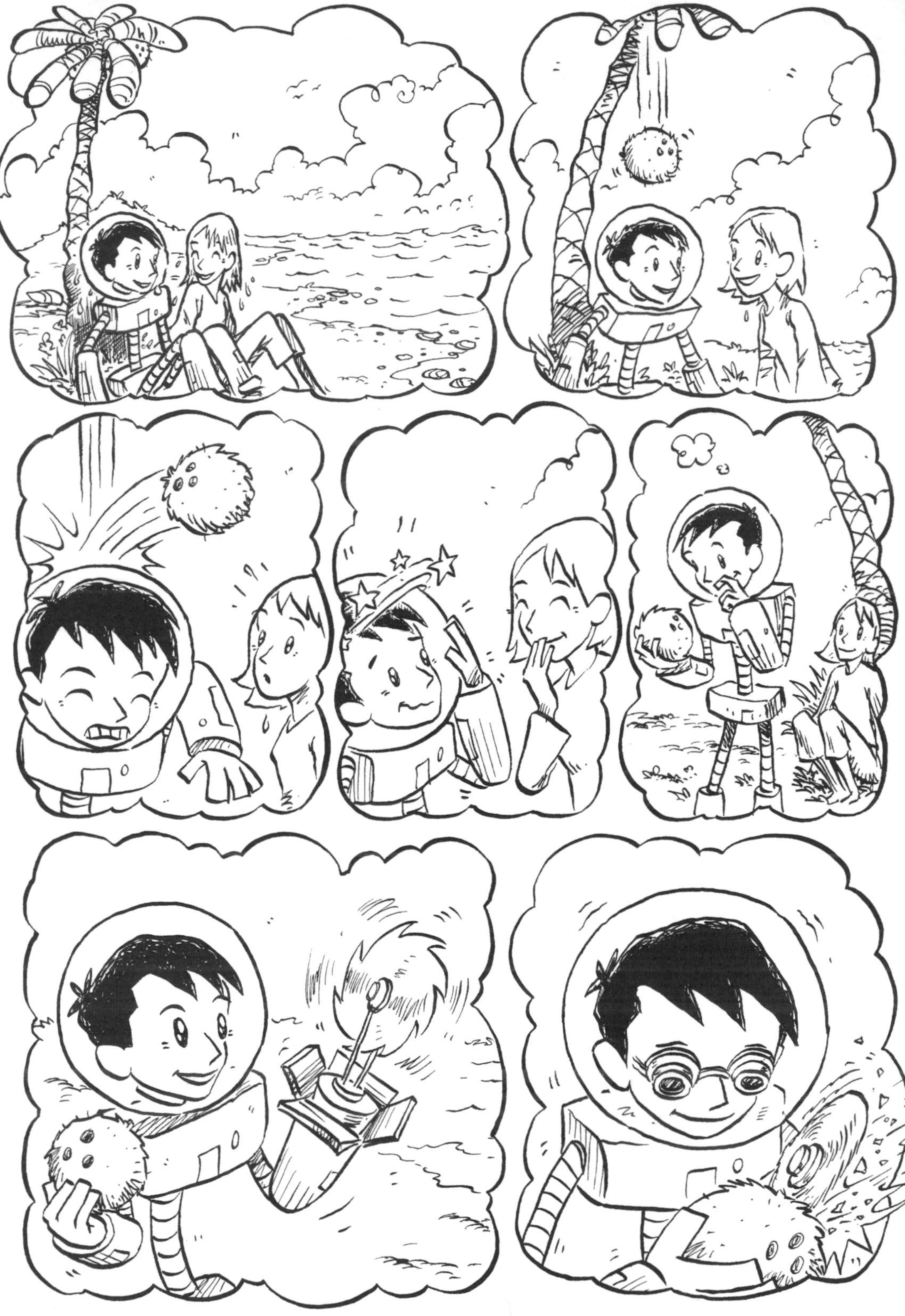

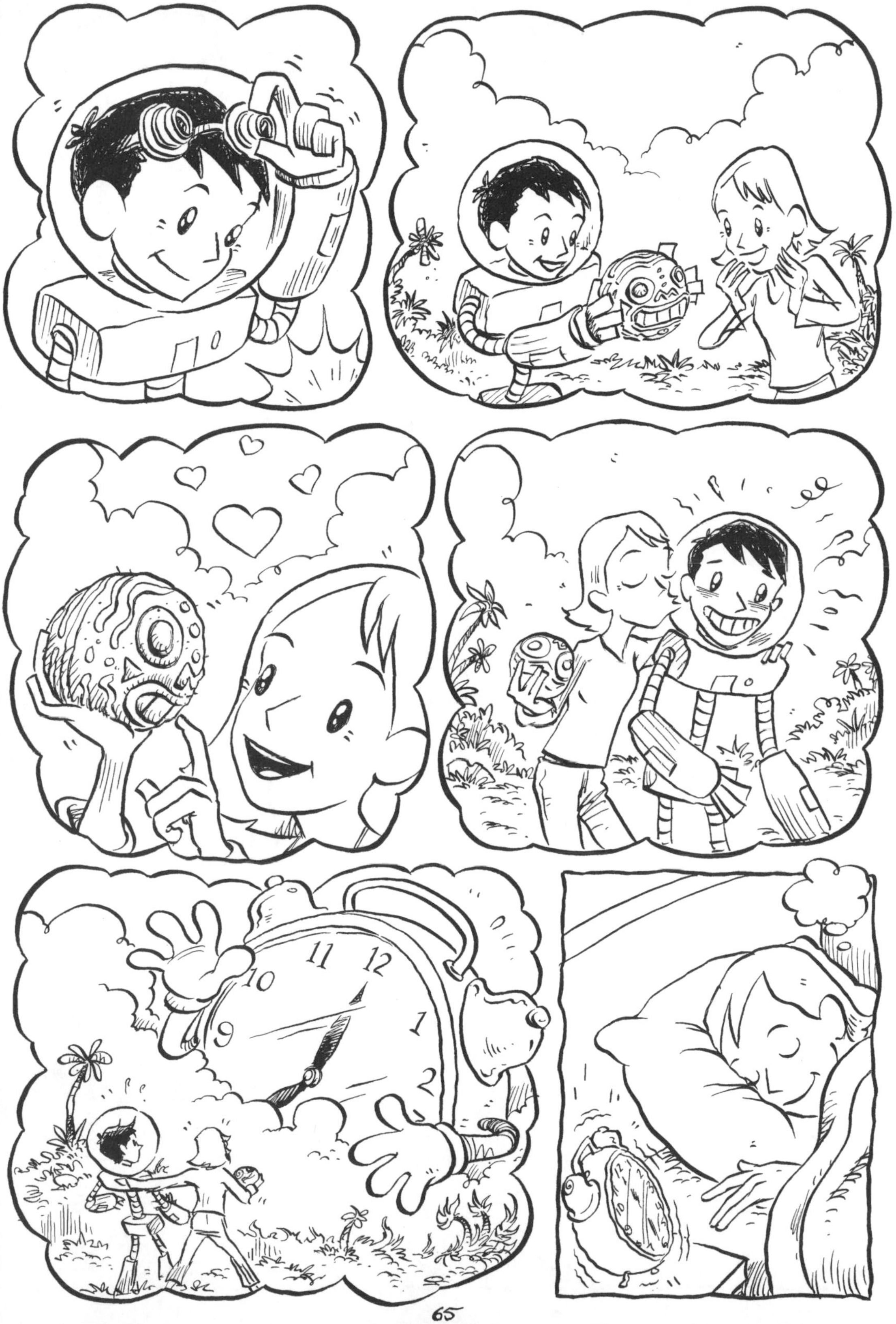

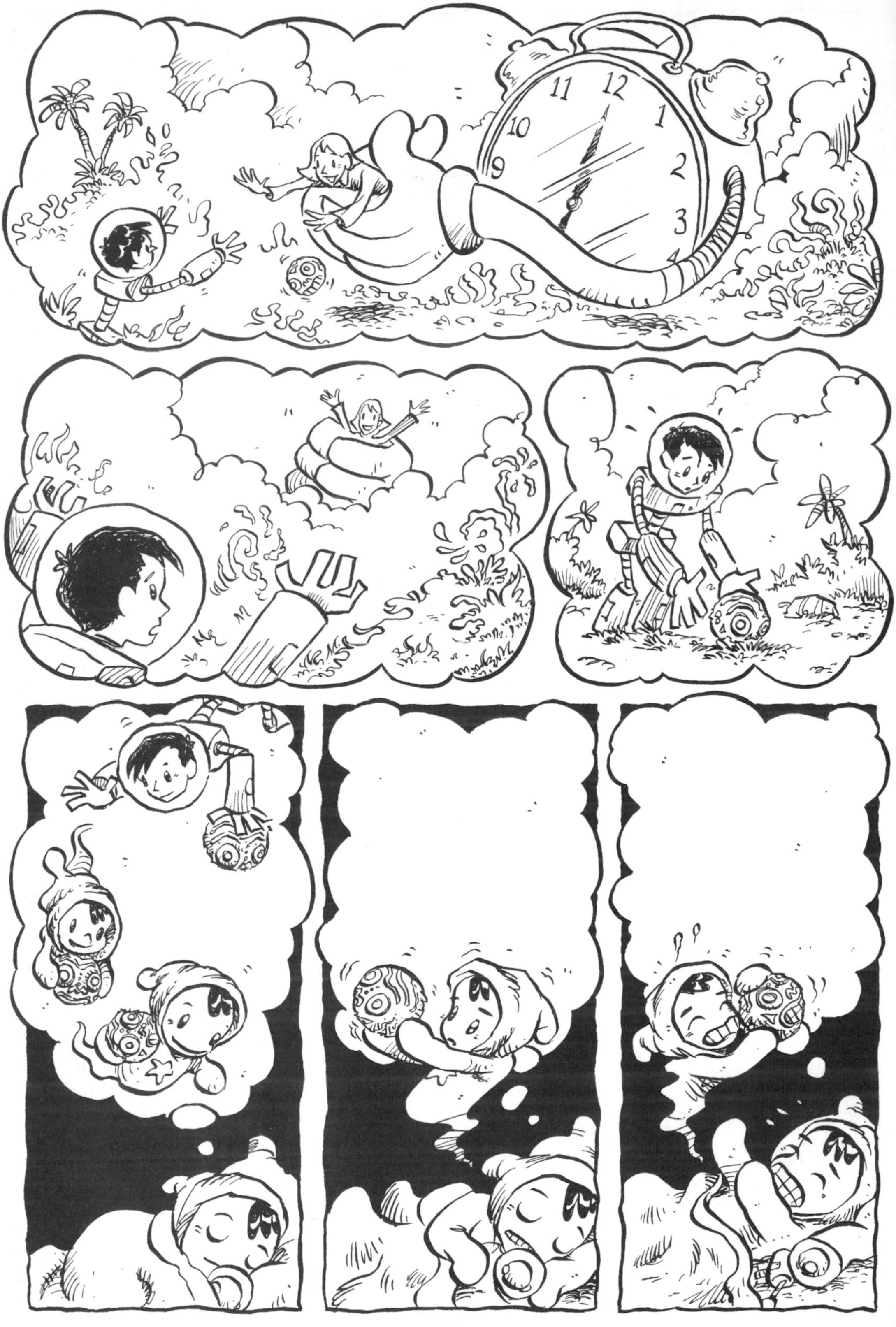

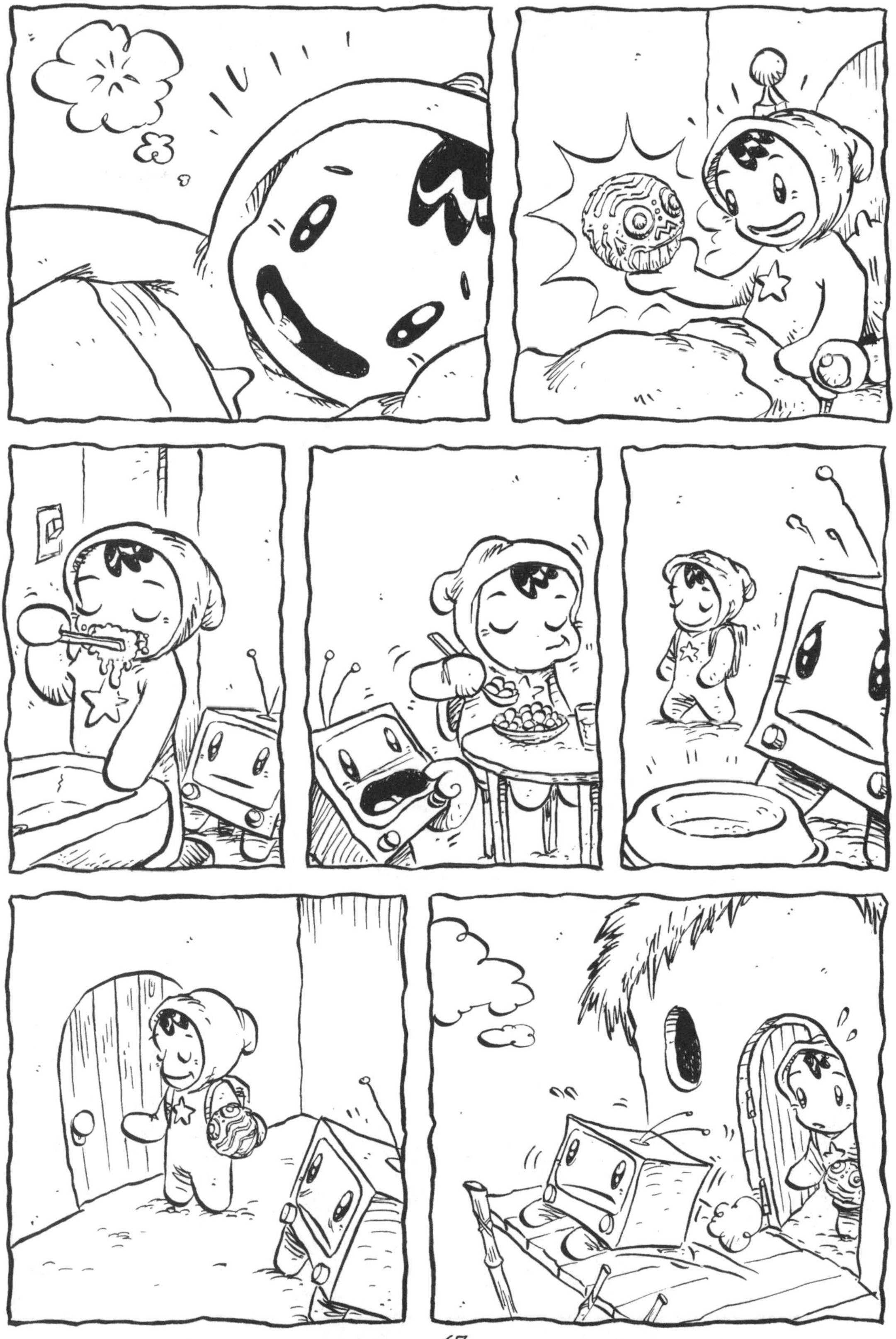

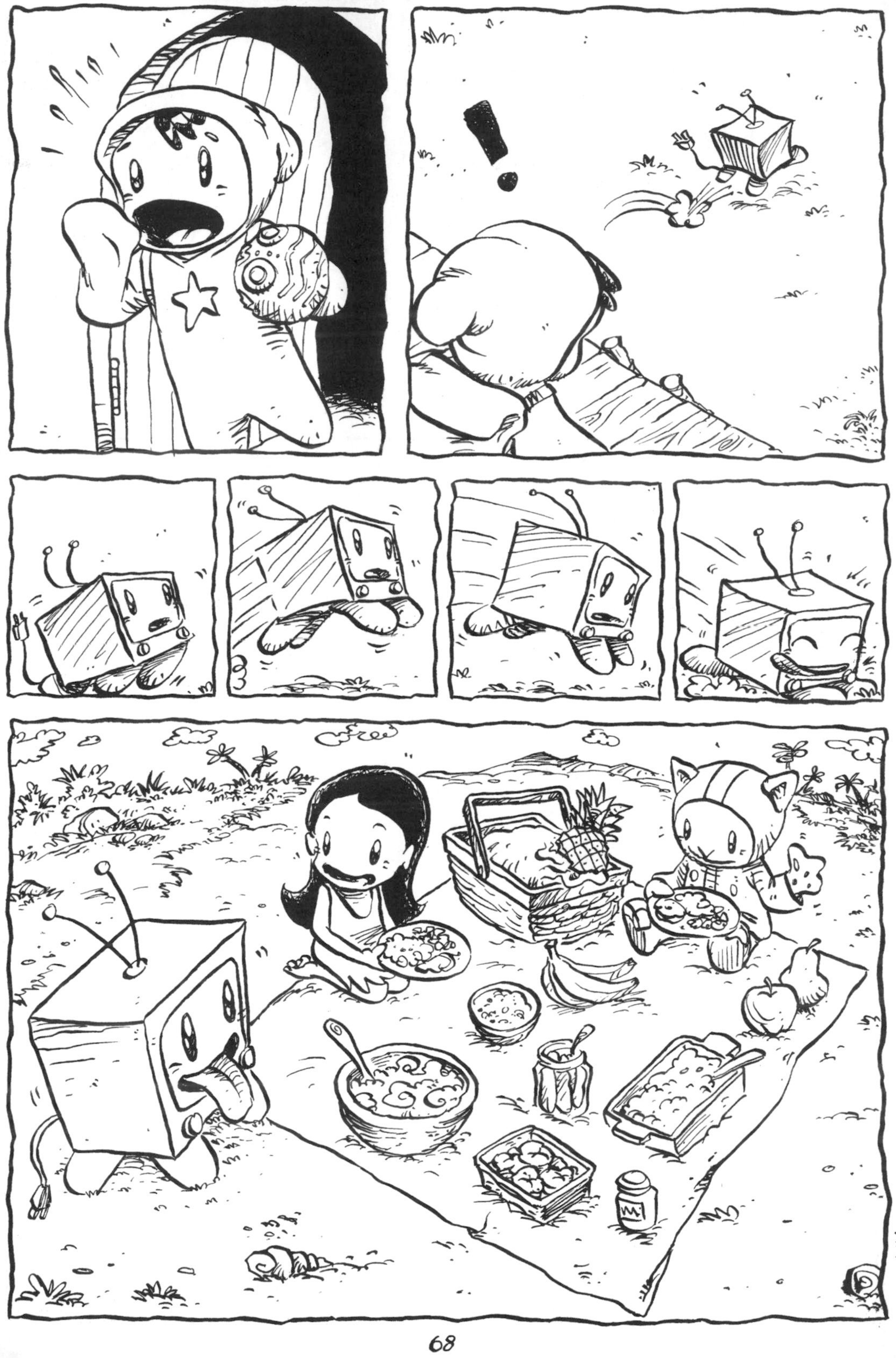
!

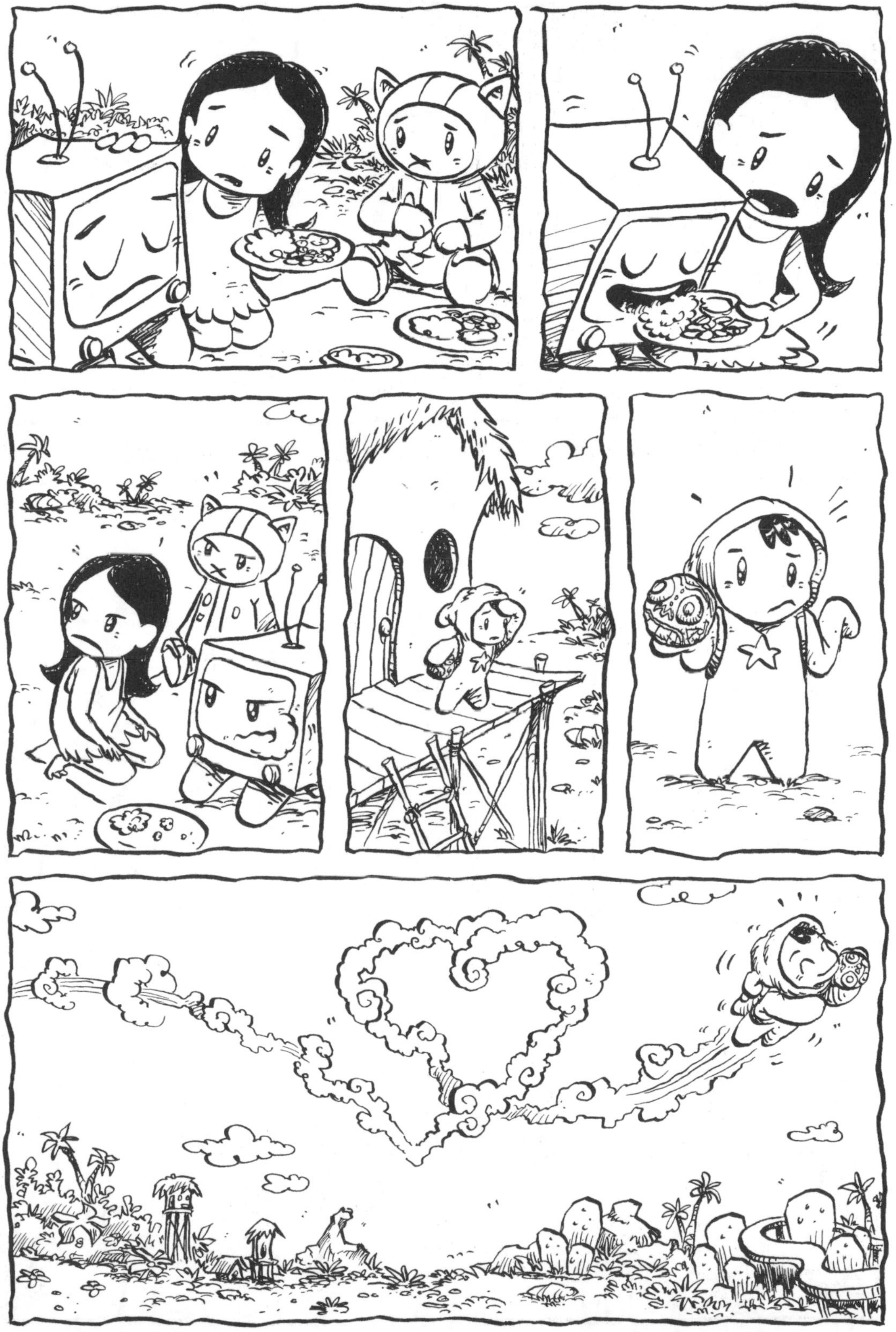

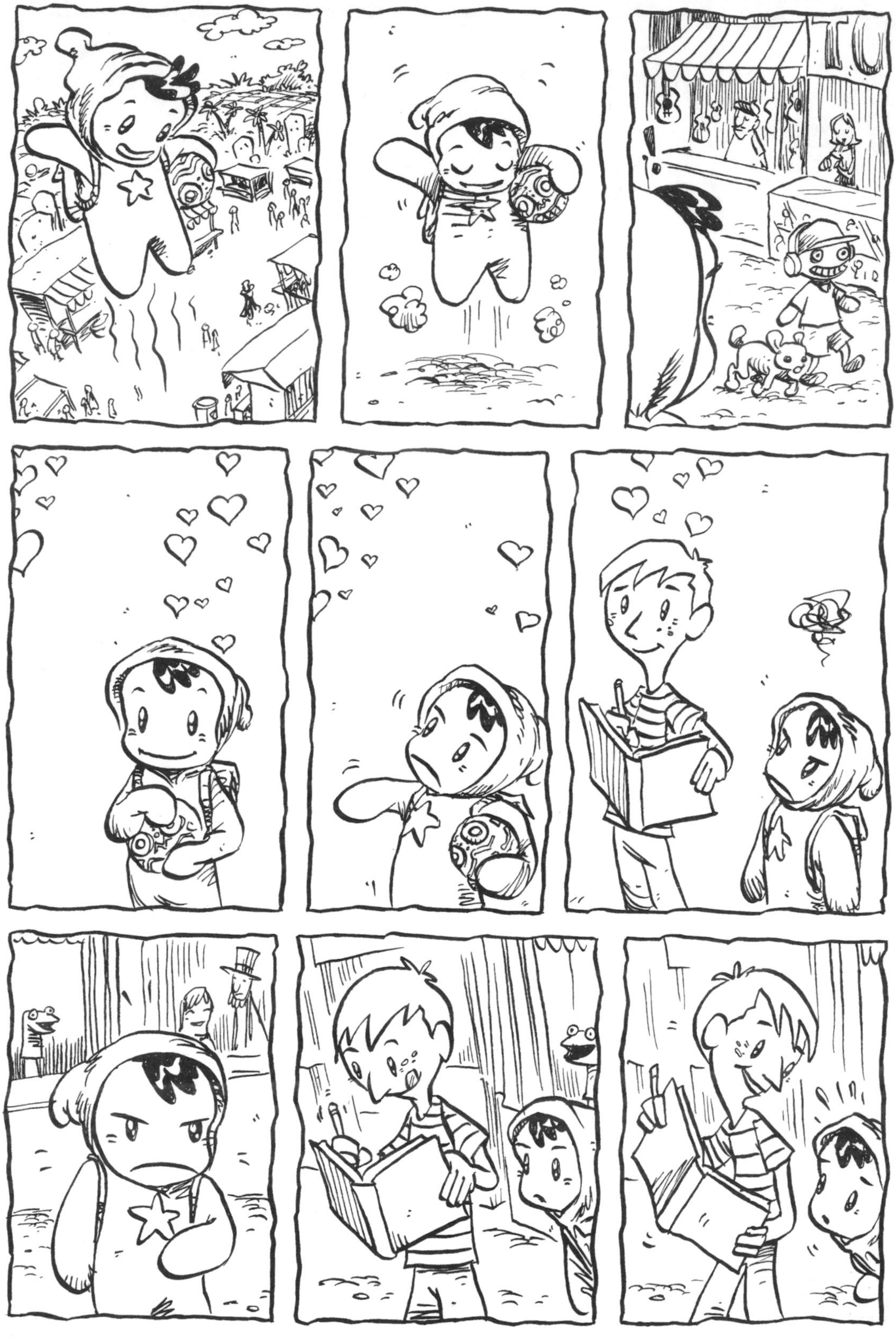

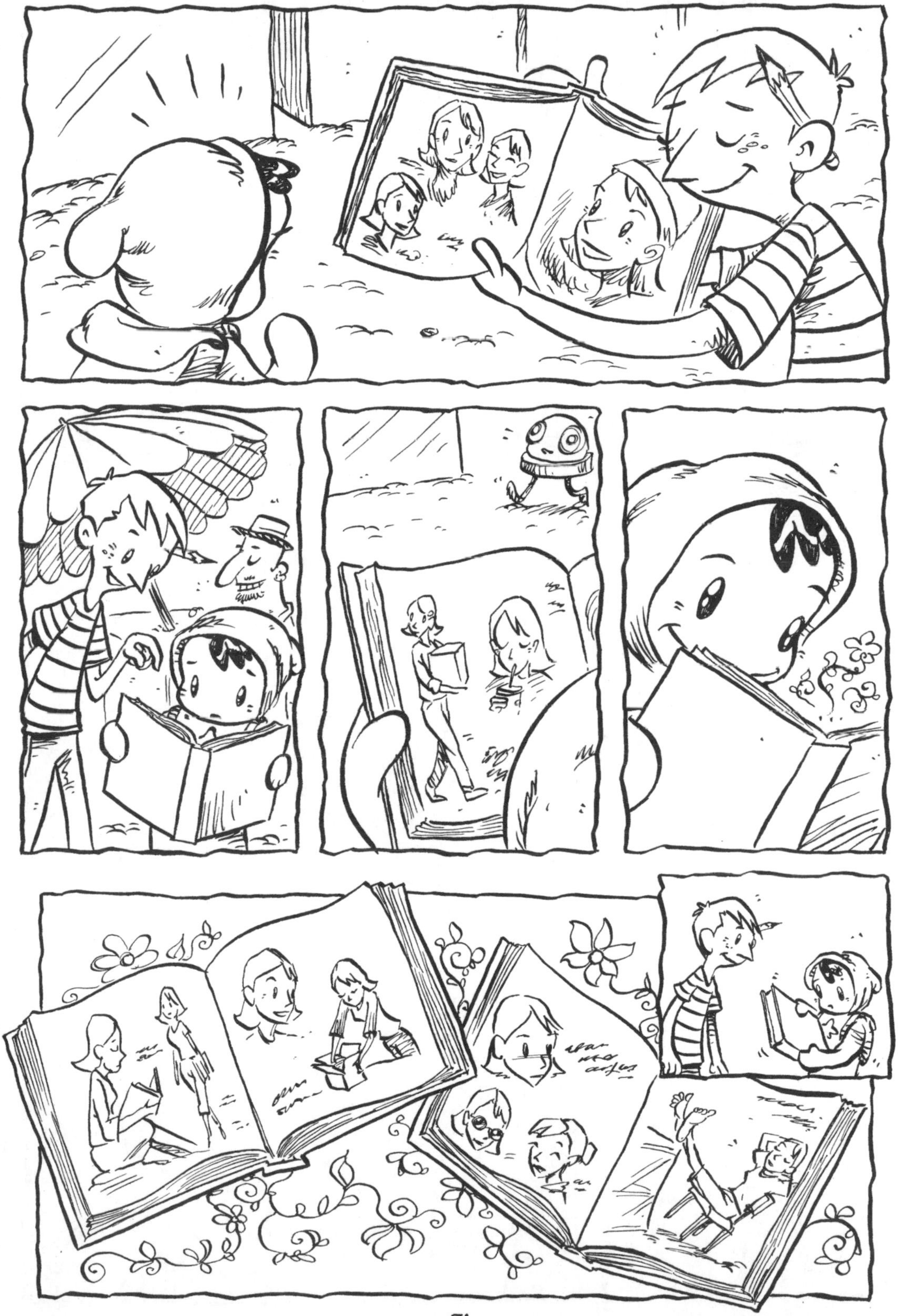

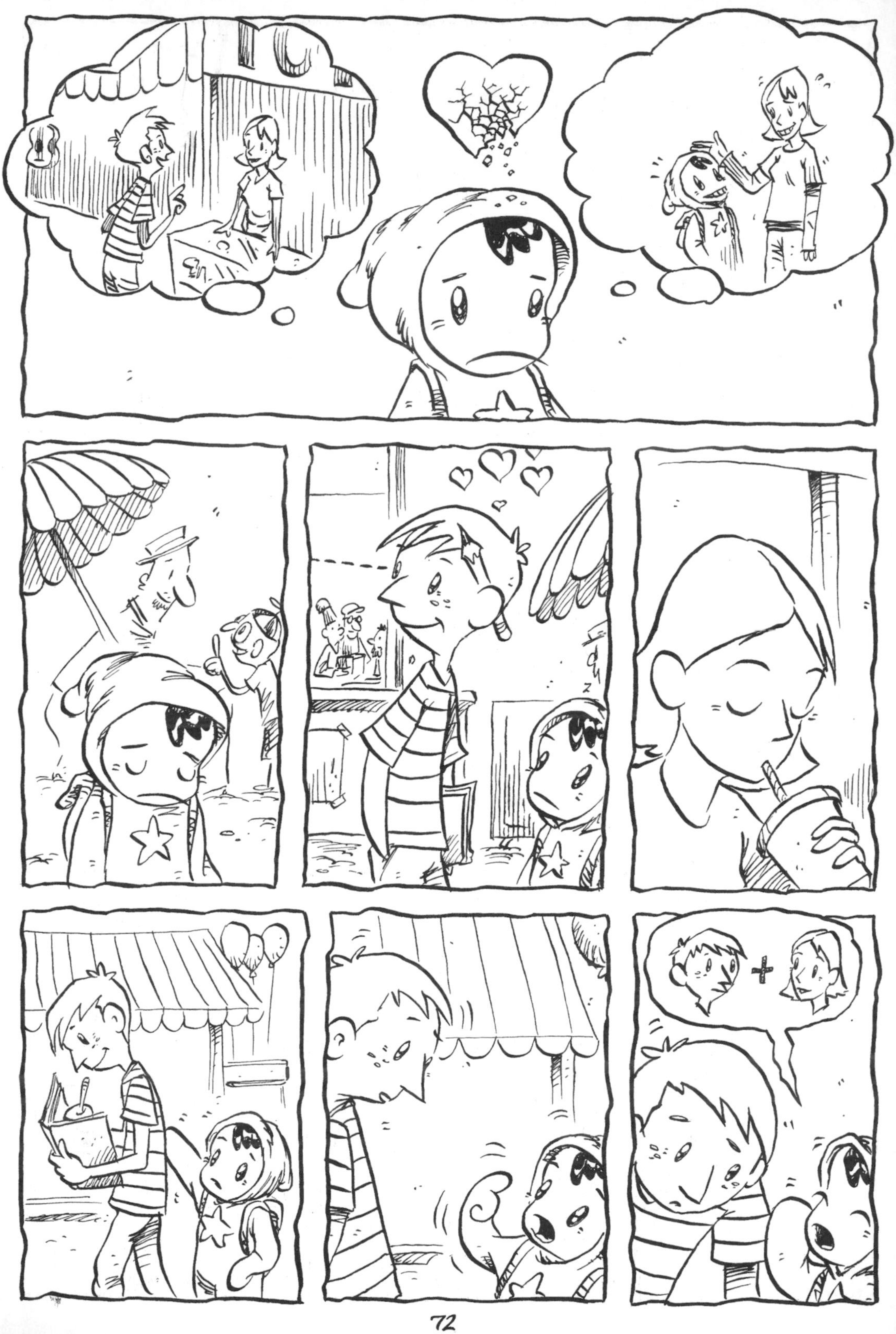

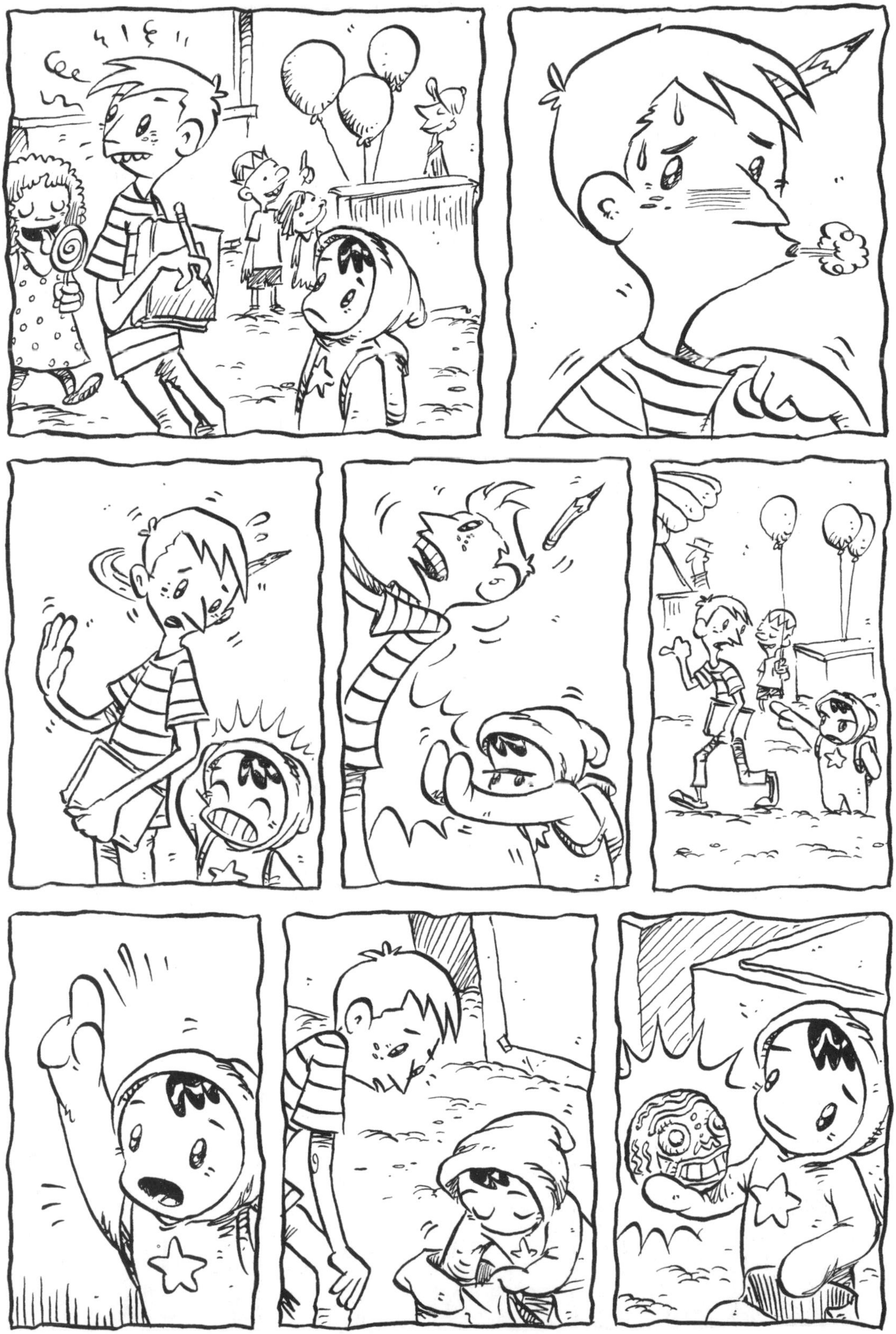

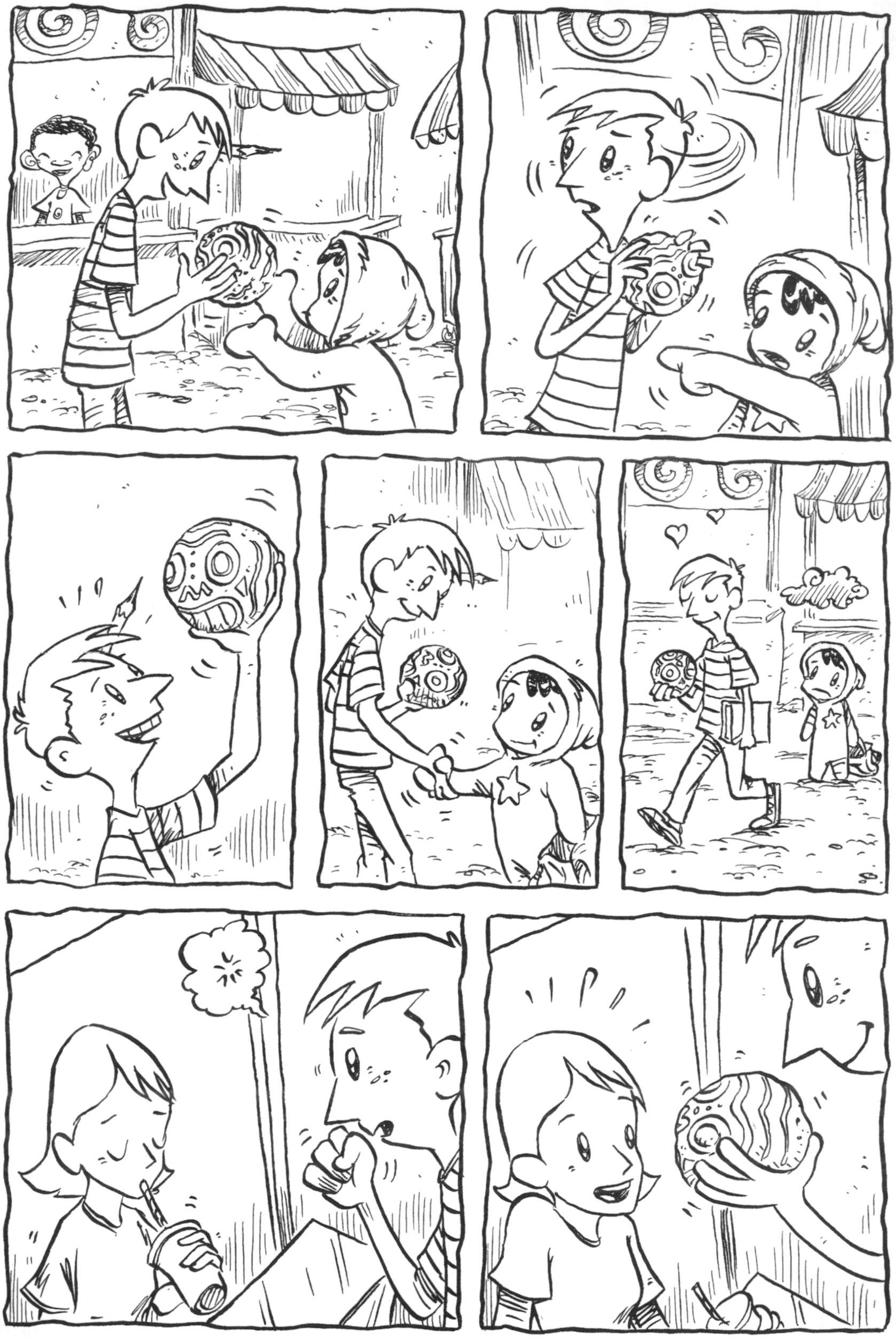

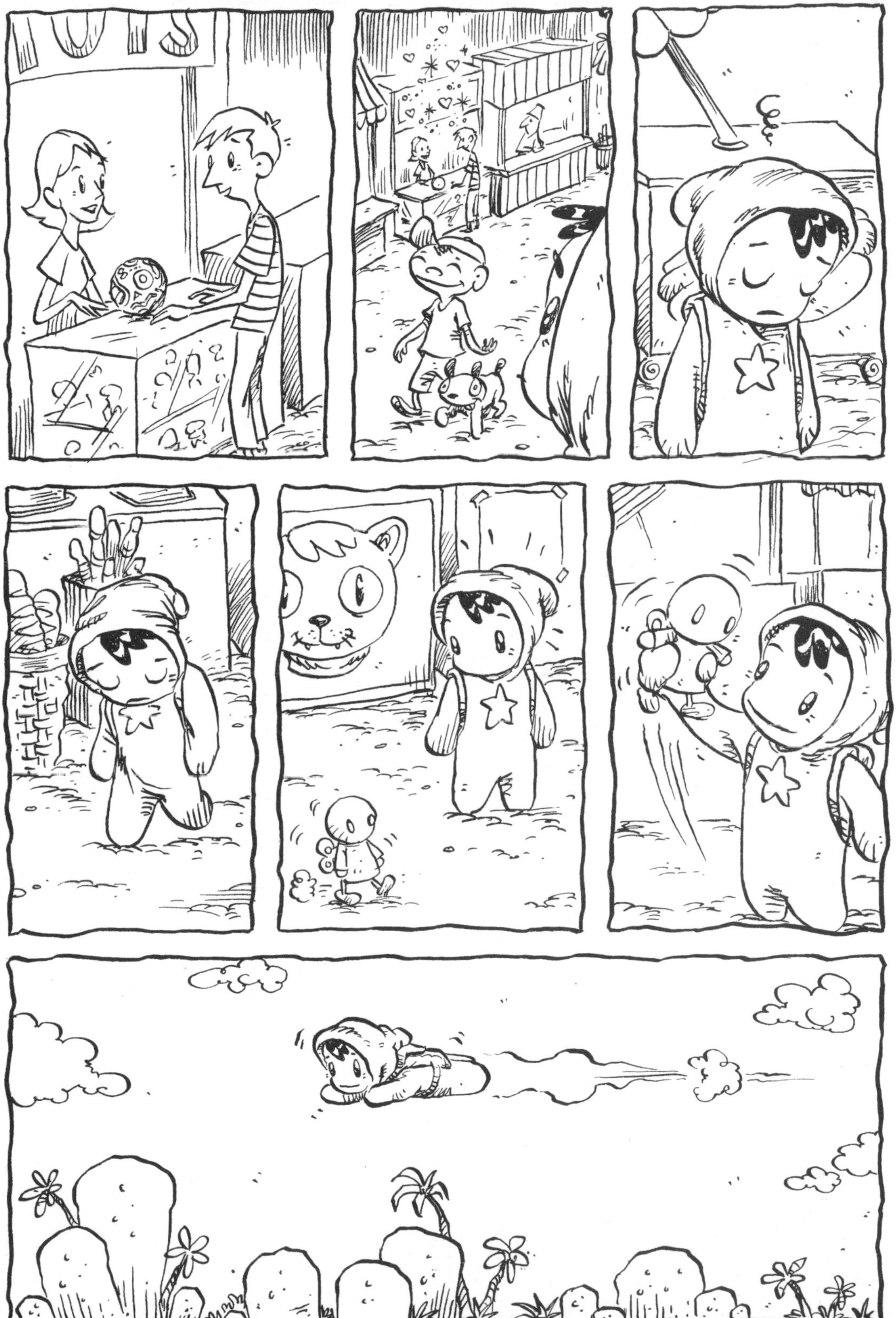

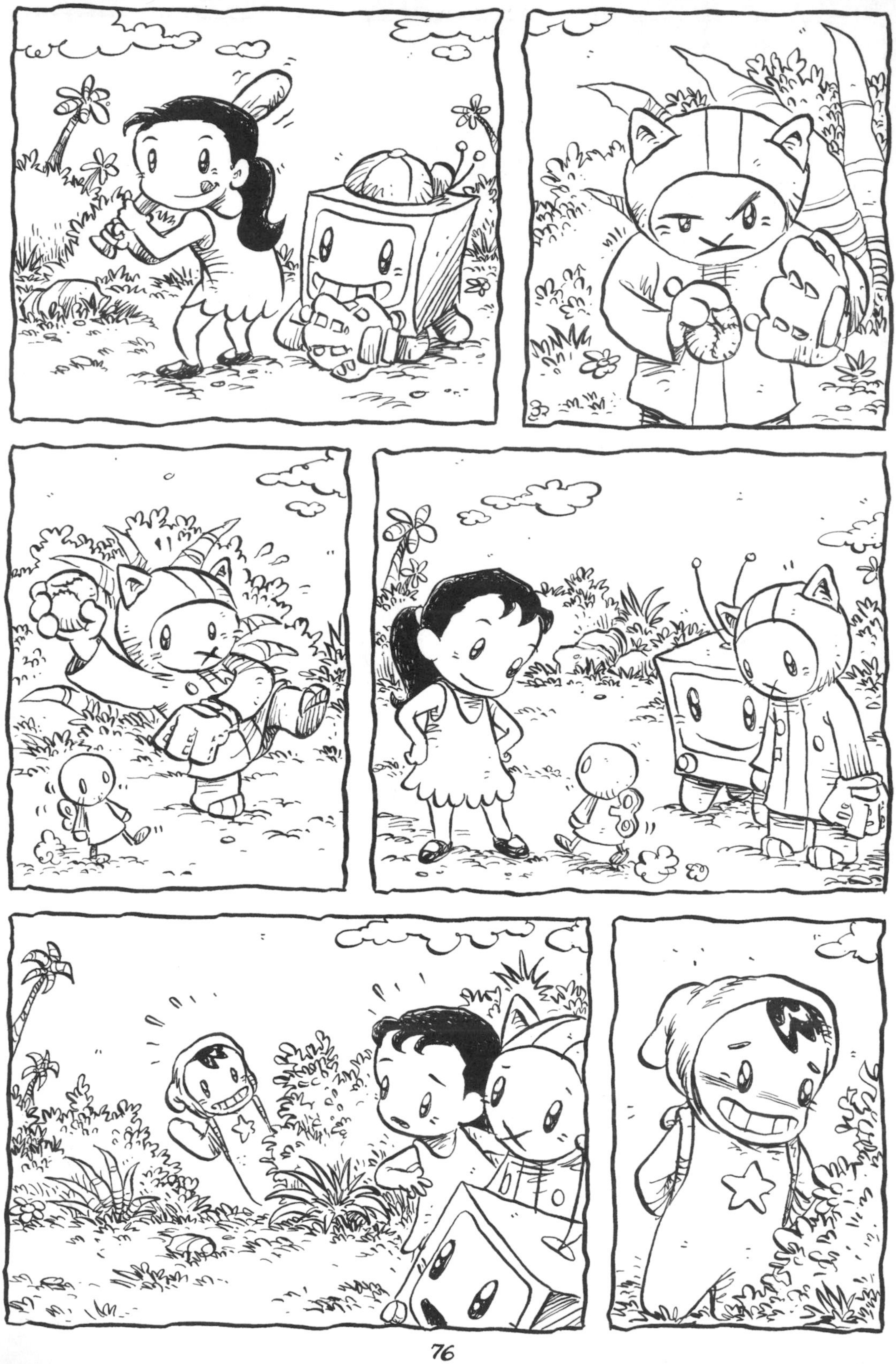

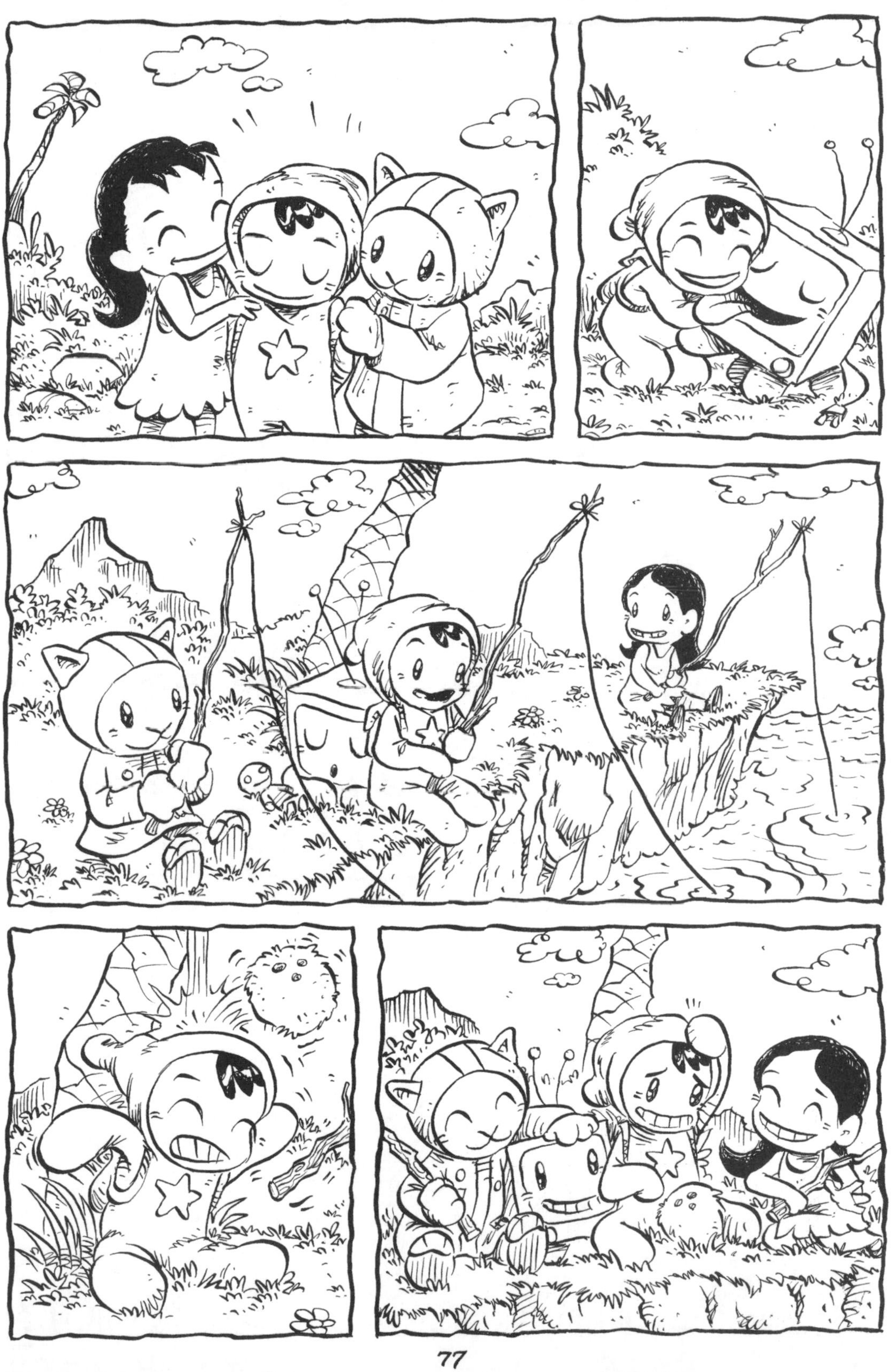

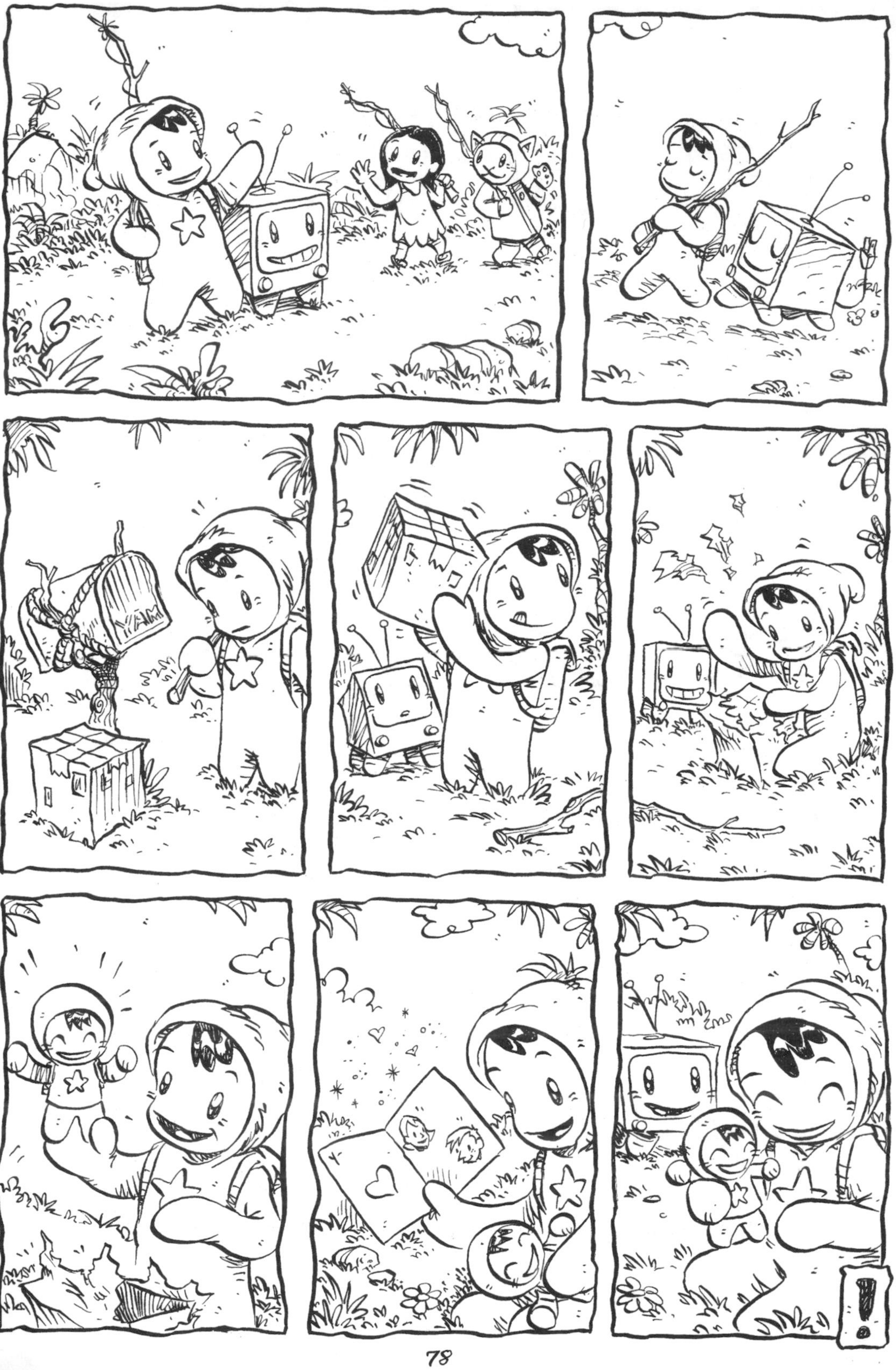
YAM
!

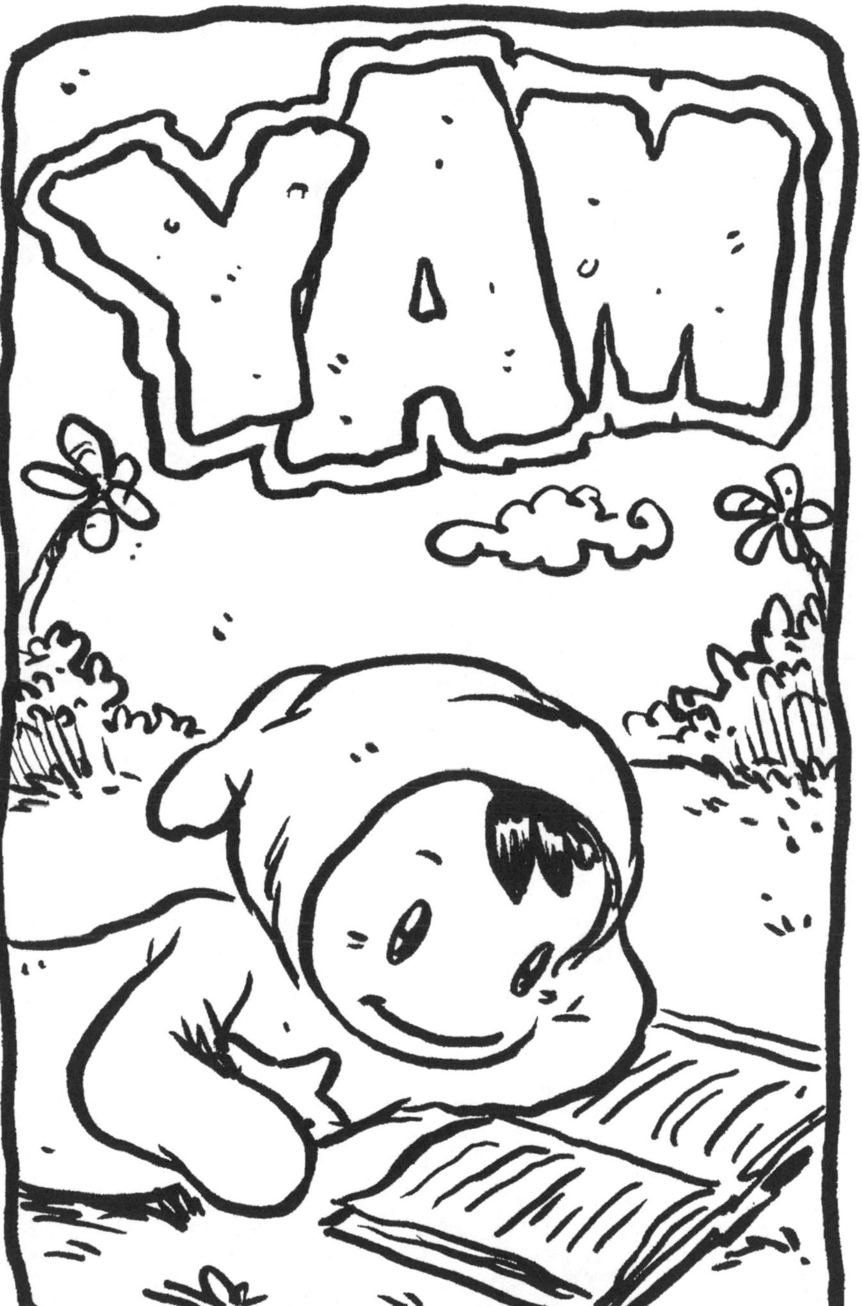
YAM

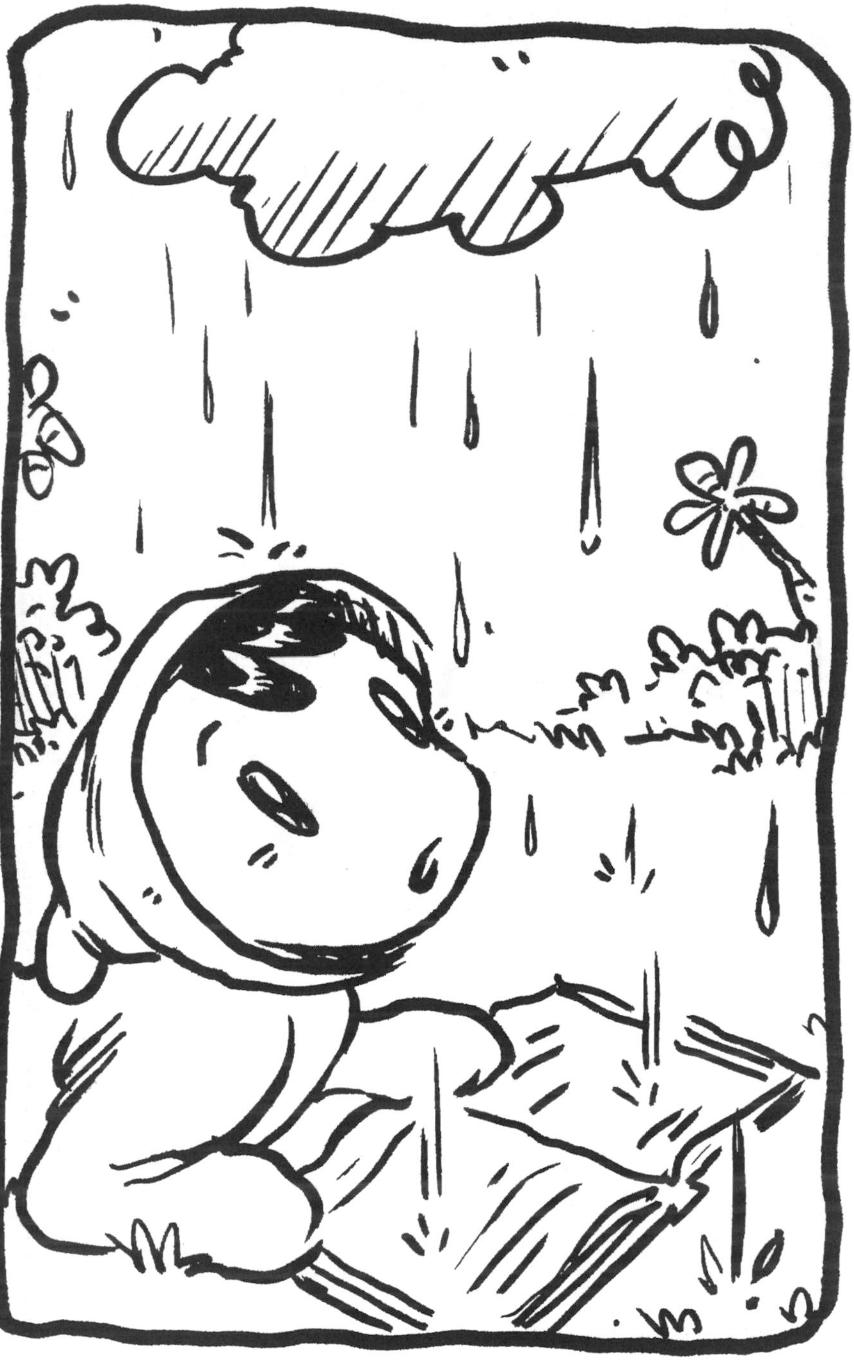

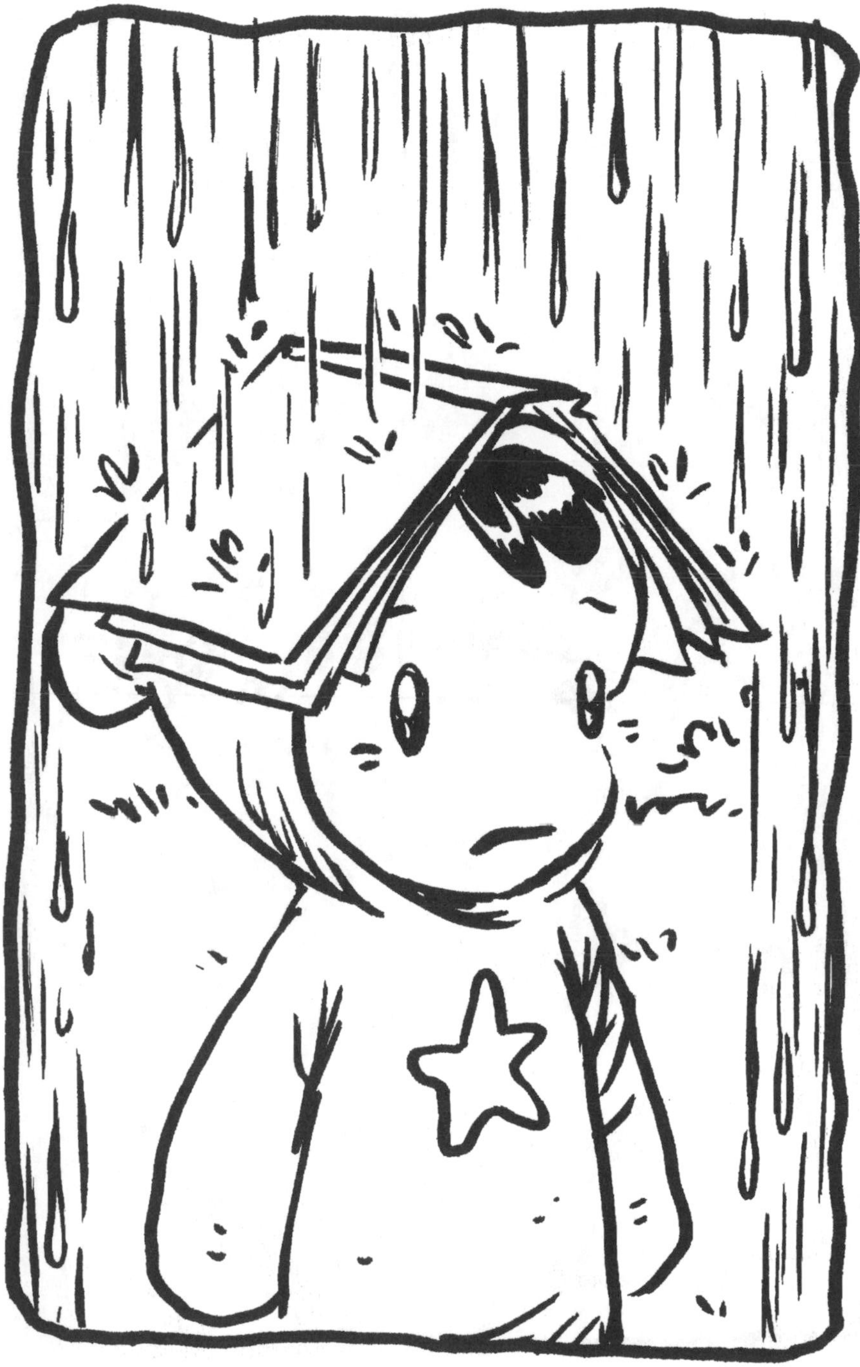

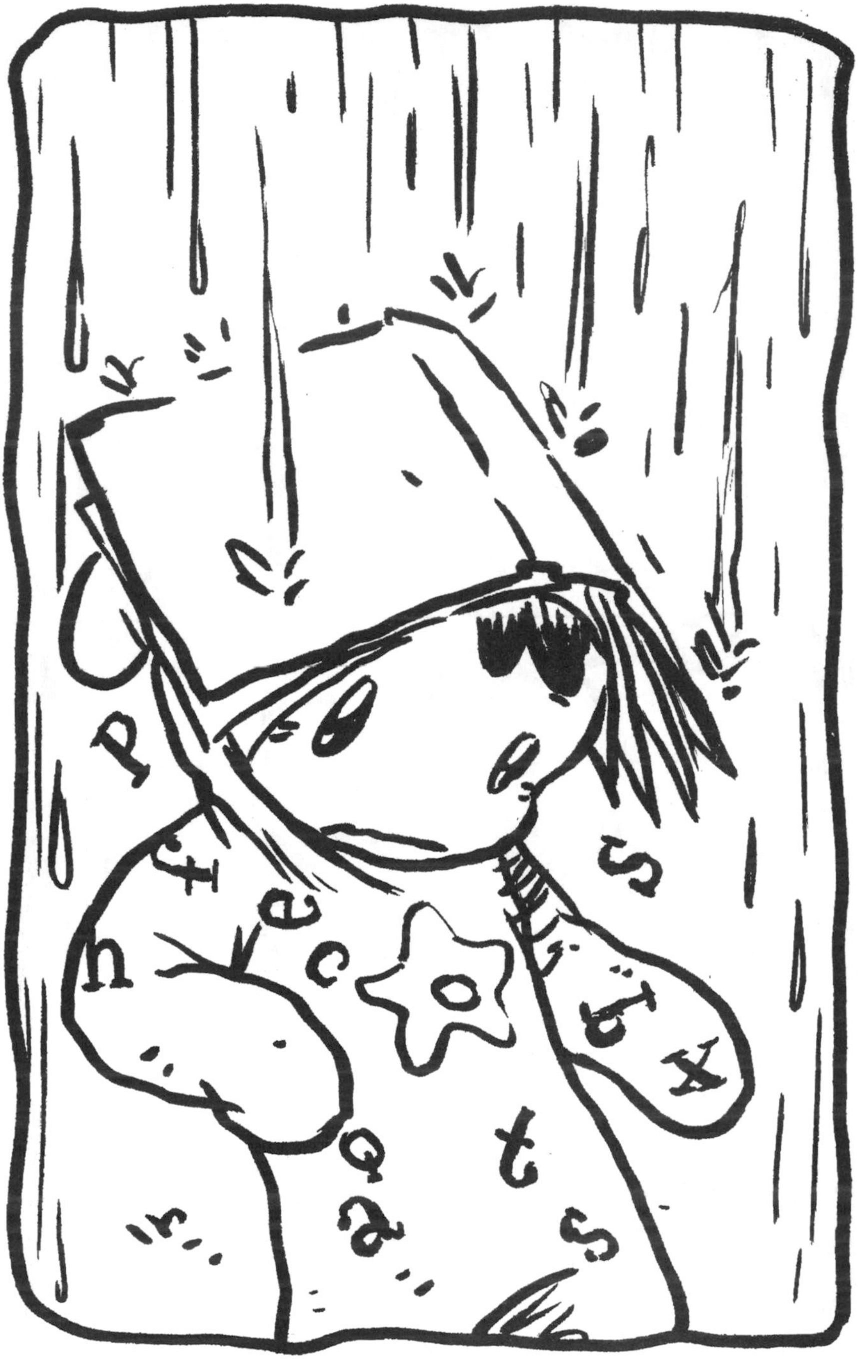

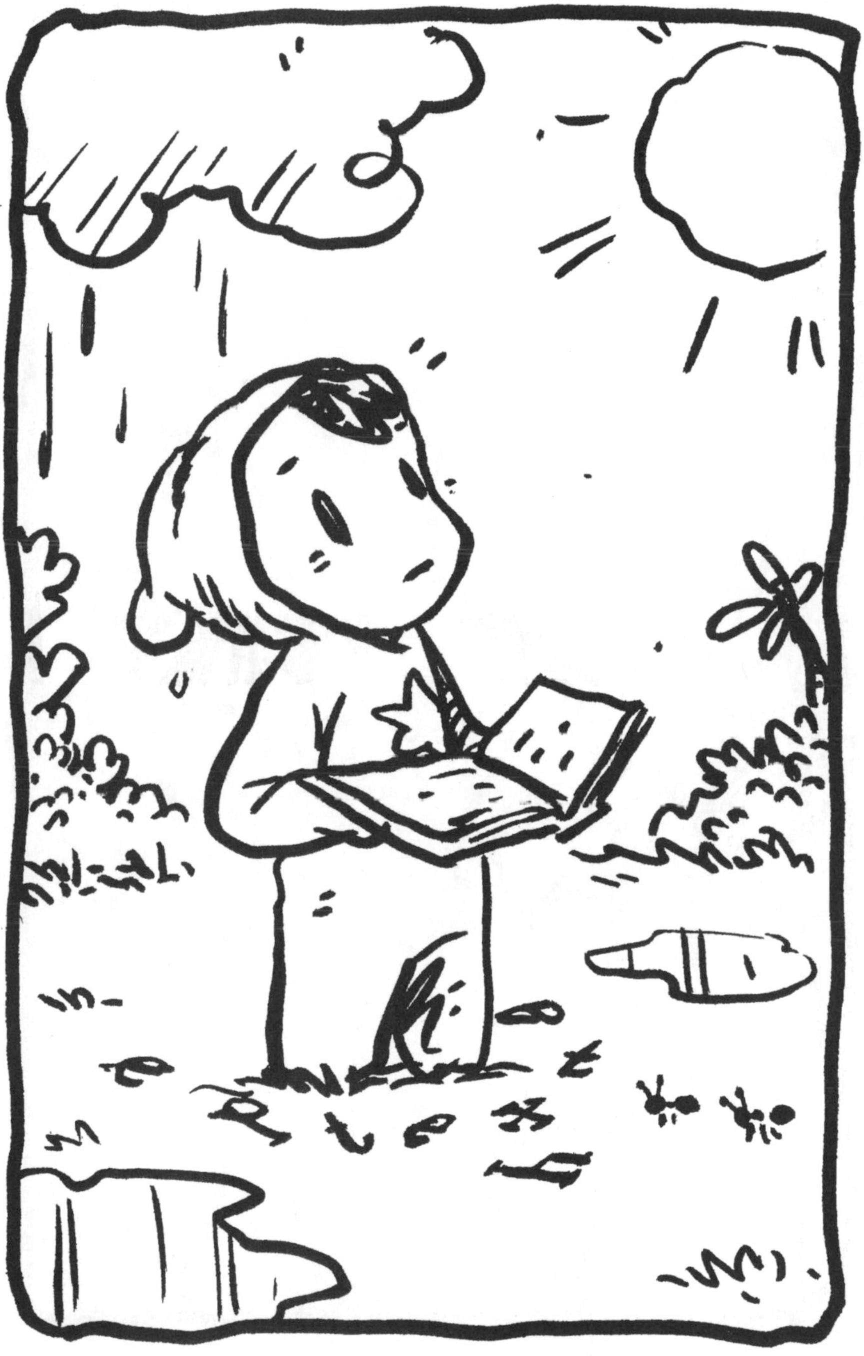

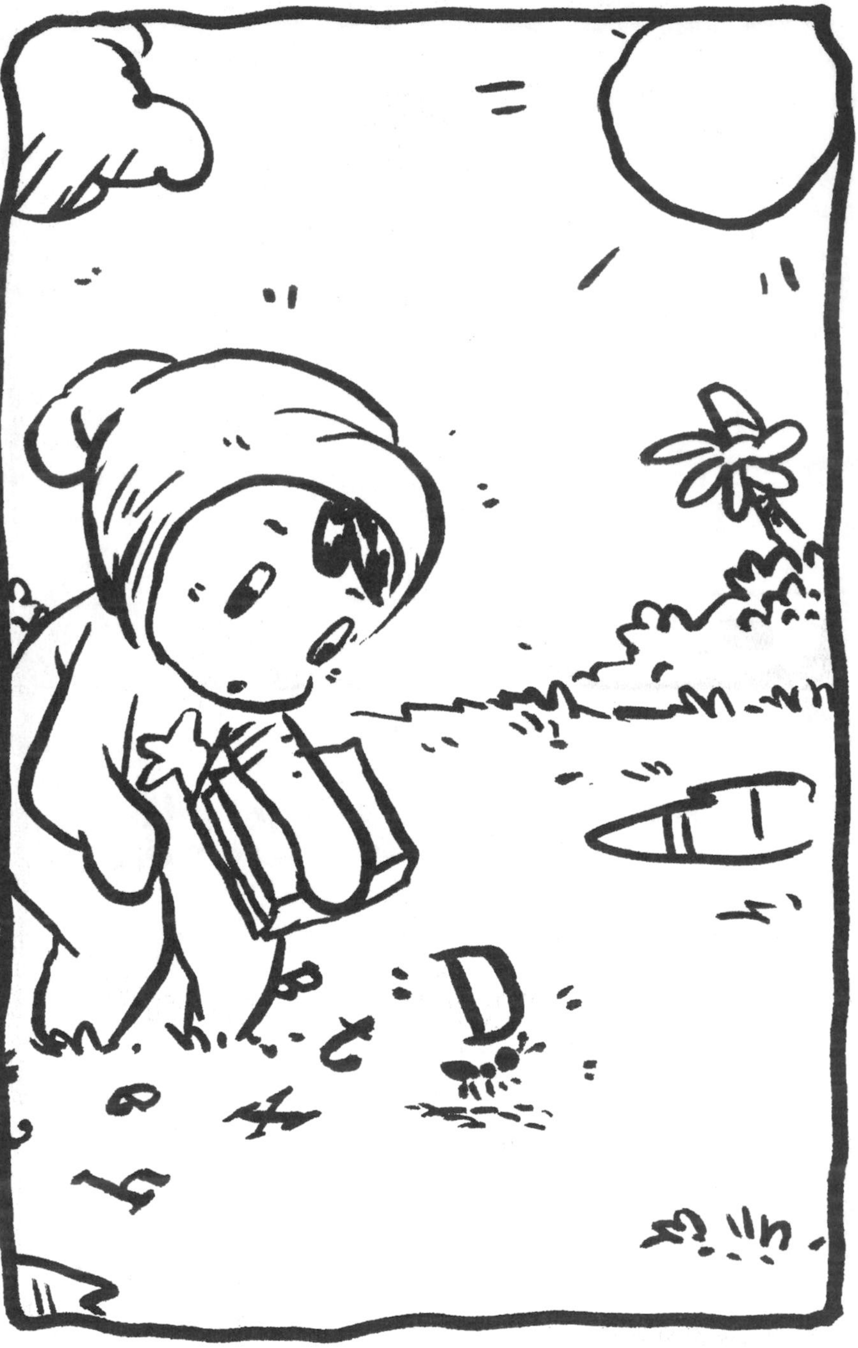

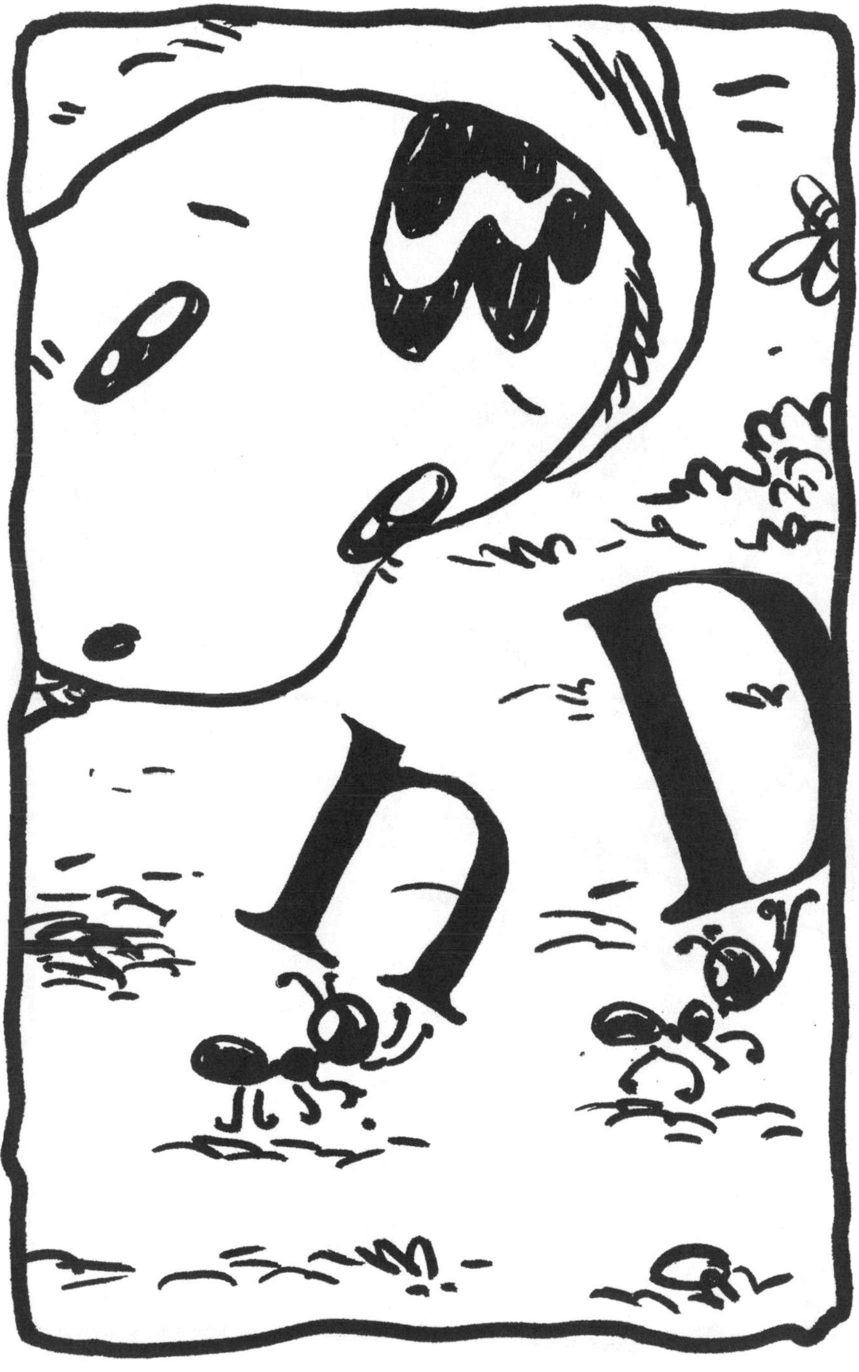

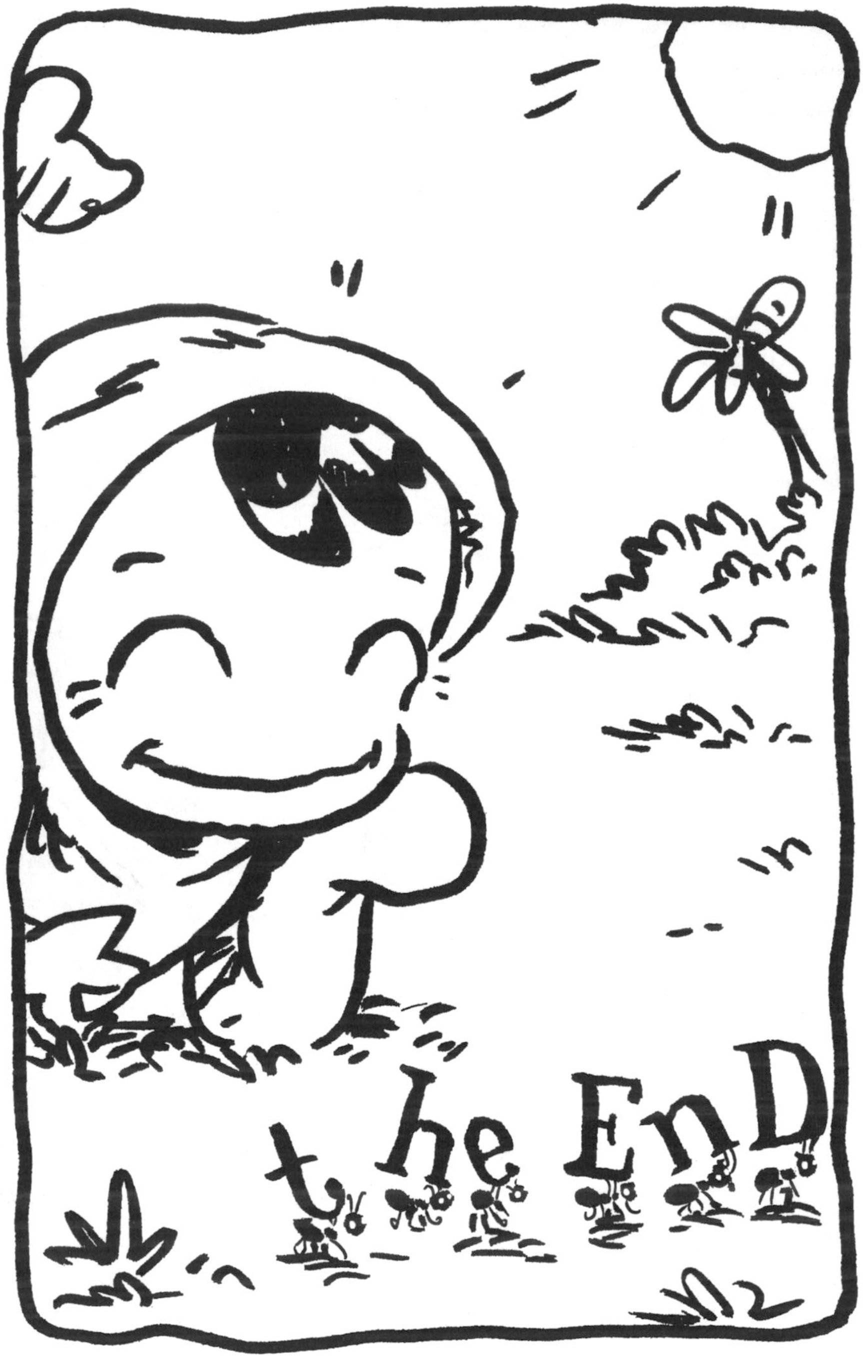
the EnD

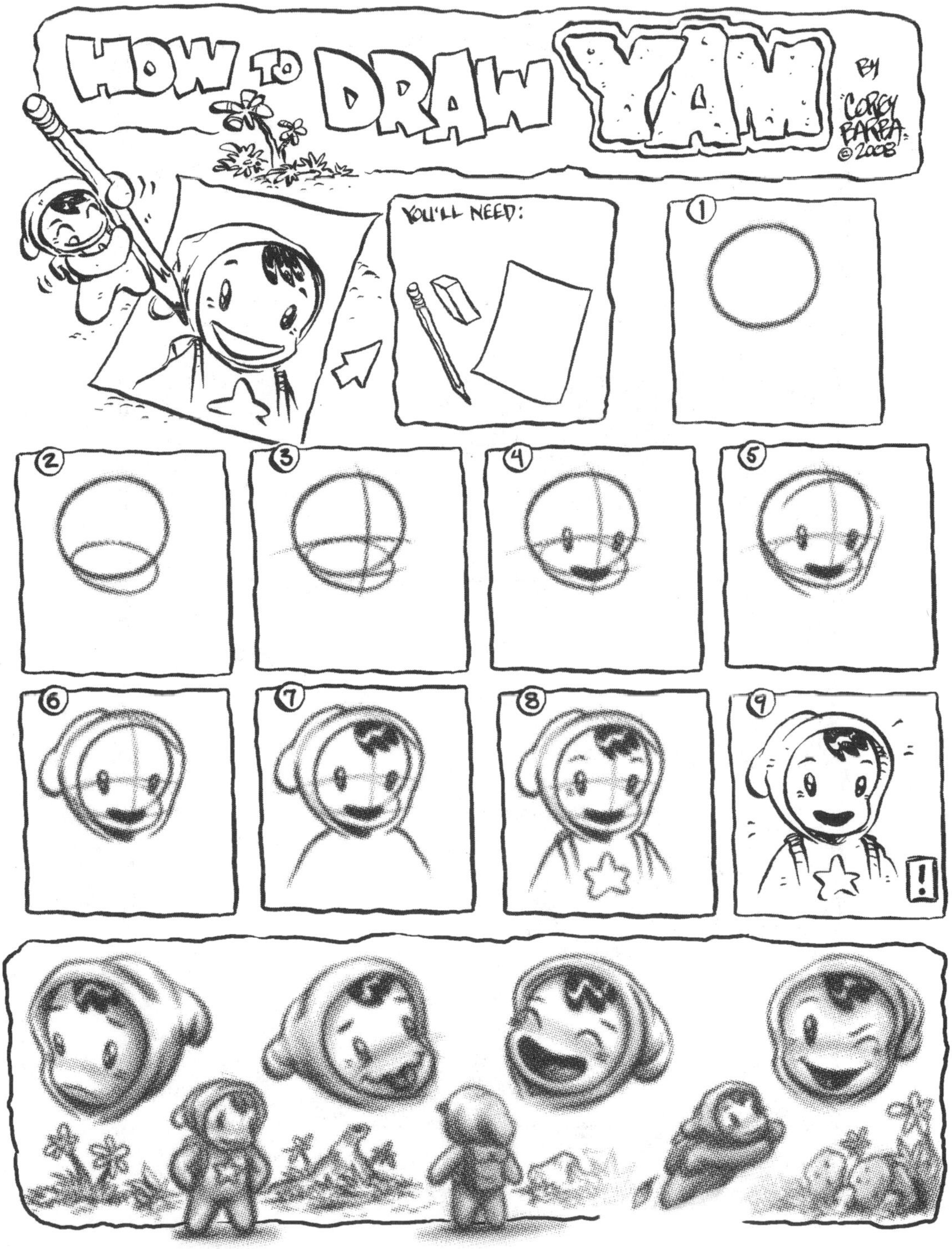
HOW TO DRAW YAM
BY COREY BARBA
© 2008
YOU'LL NEED:
1
2
3
4
5
6
7
8
9
!

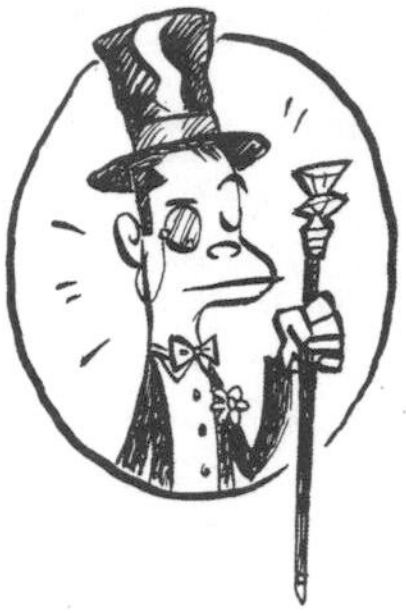

WHEN COREY BARBA WAS A BOY, HE THOUGHT HE WOULD BE A SCIENTIST OR A ROCK STAR. NOW HE IS A CARTOONIST, WHICH IS KIND OF LIKE BOTH.

COREY LIVES IN OHIO WITH HIS WIFE AND KIDS, WHERE HE ENJOYS SUSHI, TACOS AND CANDY.

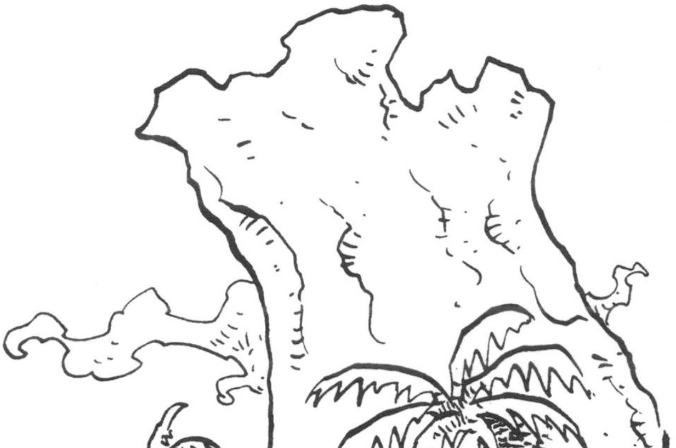

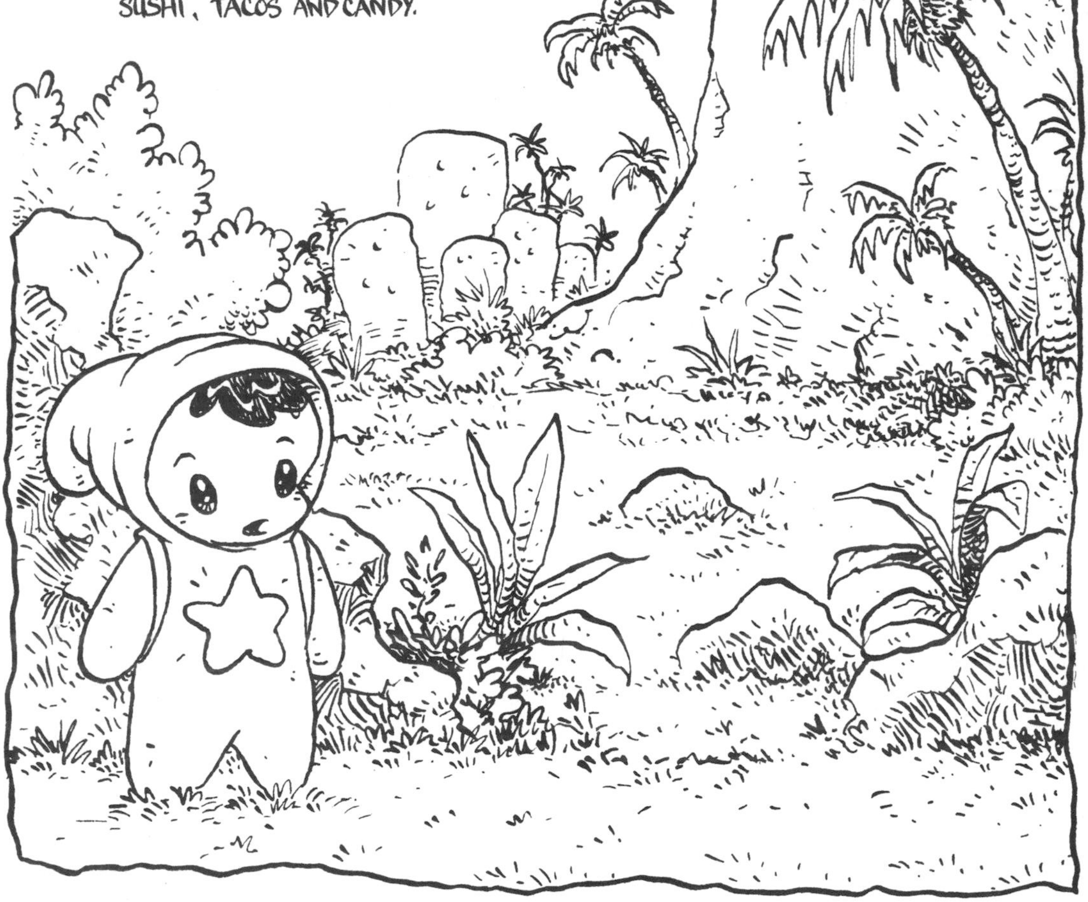